THE MAID BY MISTAKE RESCUE

TEXAS HOTLINE SERIES, BOOK #10

JO GRAFFORD

ACKNOWLEDGMENTS

Many thanks to my editor, Cathleen Weaver, and to my faithful beta readers — Mahasani, Debbie Turner, and Pigchevy. I also want to give a shout-out to my Cuppa Jo Readers on Facebook for reading and loving my books!

GET A FREE BOOK!

Join my mailing list to be the first to know about new releases, free books, special discount prices, Bonus Content, and giveaways.

https://BookHip.com/JNNHTK

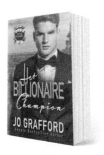

Welcome to the Texas Hotline, a team of search and rescue experts — police officers, firefighters, expert divers, and more. In an emergency, your sweet and swoon-worthy rescuer is only a phone call away.

CHAPTER 1: TRAINING CENTER NEWS

NOAH

"I was afraid it would come to this." The police chief tossed Detective Noah Zeller's leave of absence paperwork on his desk with a grunt of irritation. "Ever since that niece of mine was fool enough to break your engagement—"

"I'm not quitting," Noah cut in quickly. He'd spent the last year trying to forget the woman who'd dumped him for some rich hotshot. It hadn't been easy, though. With a police chief for an uncle and a boyfriend running for state senator, Celina had become a bit of a public figure in her own right. Nearly everything she did made headlines these days — where she went, what she wore, and who she was dating. Or no longer dating. Yeah, the story of their nasty breakup was plastered across the Internet. It was also the fodder for a stream of nonstop gossip about who each of them was dating next. The fact that Noah hadn't dated anyone since their breakup had generated endless speculation. He lived for the day when his name would finally drop out of the public's interest.

Hector Manning's mouth twisted in derision. "Who said anything about quitting?" They were standing in his spacious office in front of the wide picture window overlooking the Buffalo Bayou. The usual blur of traffic crowded the streets of downtown Houston. "This opportunity puts you on the onward and upward path. I'm the one who's going to be down an ace detective when it's all said and done."

Noah grinned as he jammed his hands into the pockets of his navy uniform trousers. "I'll only be gone a month, sir." He saw no need to act like someone was dying.

"Right." The chief snorted. "You think I don't know how this works? I'm well aware that the Texas Hotline Training Center only recruits the nation's finest. That means the biggest employers with the biggest budgets will be circling like sharks to snap you up the moment you graduate."

"I already have a good job," Noah assured, trying not to laugh. As the most populous city in Texas, Houston wasn't exactly small beans. He couldn't believe his boss was making such a big deal out of nothing.

"They'll offer you a better one." Hector Manning pivoted in his black patent leather shoes and stomped back to his desk. "And there's nothing to keep you here when they do. No family. No—"

"Nothing but a jam-packed caseload," Noah interrupted. *Thanks to you.* Right now, his top priority was a high-profile missing persons case. "I gave my word to Bram Carstens that I would locate his granddaughter, and I'm a man of my word."

The terminally ill shipping tycoon had already been the victim of not one, but two, criminal imposter schemes. Though both fake granddaughters were now behind bars, he and his team of estate attorneys were constantly being battered with false hope concerning the whereabouts of his real grand-daughter. So far, even the promise of a hefty mone-tary reward hadn't been enough to bring any real witnesses forward on the tip line.

The fact that Bram Carstens was running out of time was the only downside to Noah's acceptance at the Texas Hotline Training Center. He'd just have to find a way to continue working the case while he was away.

The police chief took a seat in his swivel chair and rapped his knuckles against his solid wood desk-top. "Although it's not a popular theory with ol' Bram and his attorneys, you and I both know there's a chance Farrah Carstens is no longer alive."

Noah pivoted to face his boss. "Anything's possible." As a man of faith, though, he generally hoped for the best outcomes in his cases, right up to the point where there was no longer any reason to continue hoping.

"I hate to point out the obvious, but she has more relatives who'd want her dead than alive."

"So the tabloids claim." The social rags treated the Carstens family like royalty. And, for all intents and purposes, they were. Their shipping dynasty possessed deep enough pockets to buy and sell small countries. Sadly, their wealth made every potential heir a target. After mulling over the case day and night for the past month, however, Noah's gut was telling him that the long-lost Carstens granddaughter was very much still breathing. He was currently leaning toward another possibility — that she didn't want to be found.

"You don't sound very convinced." The police chief leaned back in his chair, looking disgruntled.

"What can I say?" Noah shrugged. "I'm a cup-half-full kind of guy." He preferred to keep an open mind. All too often, the most popular theories and opinions ended up sorely debunked.

"I don't see why, in this case." Hector Manning threw his hands in the air. "Farrah Carstens would have to be living under a rock to miss the media frenzy over her current whereabouts."

"Or off the grid," Noah mused. "Some people have their reasons for unplugging themselves from society." Self-preservation alone would be enough to keep Farrah Carstens out of the public's eye.

Though the police had been blasting the news channels with computerized renderings of what she might've looked like at every stage, from birth until the present, the sketches had produced nothing but crickets. It was odd. Someone really should have come forward by now. Someone who'd known her as a child, perhaps — a teacher, a coach, anyone. The fact that they hadn't come forward suggested one of two options. She was either dead, as many people believed her to be, or her appearance had been deliberately altered at an early age. From Noah's angle, that was an awful lot of trouble to go to on behalf of someone who was not intended to live a good long life.

Yep. Farrah Carstens was most likely alive, and he intended to prove it.

His boss studied him through narrowed lids. "I recognize that look. Makes me think you know something you're not telling me."

"It's only a theory, sir." One that Noah fully planned to take with him to the Texas Hotline Training Center. His brain worked even when he was sleeping. He couldn't disengage it from the case if he tried. If there was any time at all at the training center, he would continue to review the missing woman's case files and follow up on every lead.

After a long pause, Police Chief Manning nodded grimly. "It goes without saying, but I'll say it, anyway. I'll push any material evidence your way the moment it surfaces."

"I'll do the same, sir."

His boss gave a dry chuckle. "I doubt you'll be doing anything but training at the center, but okay." He stood and thrust out a hand.

Noah strode across the room to clasp it. "I really am coming back, sir." Ever since the death of Noah's great-uncle, who'd dragged him out of the foster care system, he'd considered the police chief to be the closest thing he had to a father figure. Though it wasn't something they'd ever talked about, the guy had to know Noah felt that way about him. He was too smart not to know.

Hector Manning briefly tightened his grip on Noah's hand. "I know I sound like a broken record, but I'm truly sorry about how things ended between you and my niece."

"Me, too." Noah dropped the guy's hand. He wouldn't have minded being related by marriage to the police chief, definitely wouldn't have minded having a family again. If Noah was being honest with himself, it was his biggest regret over things not working out with Celina. *Shoot!* It was no wonder she'd broken things off with him. He wanted a family almost more than he wanted a girl-friend. A diva like her would've picked up on that sentiment and resented not being the center of his attention.

He left the chief's office without another word. Since he only lived a few blocks from work, he hadn't bothered driving his pickup truck. It was less than a ten-minute walk to his top-level studio apartment, and most of that time was spent waiting at the two stoplights on his way there.

He'd managed to negotiate a pretty sweet setup at the upscale community of high-rises where he lived. In exchange for a fully furnished crash pad that was professionally cleaned on a weekly basis, he allowed them to use his place for Monday through Saturday tours of the facility. His minimalistic life-style was a perfect fit for their showroom needs.

As it turned out, a tour of his apartment was in progress when he arrived at his door. He loitered in the sun-drenched hallway until it was finished. The forty-ish property manager flipped a handful of her platinum blonde hair over her shoulder at the sight of him. Clacking his way in a navy suit and siren-red stilettos, she batted her lashes. "You're home early, detective."

He refused to look down at the hand she placed on his forearm, knowing she was flirting. Again. "I'm heading out of town," he informed her blandly.

"Oh?" Her red-painted lips twisted into a pout.

"My boss is shipping me away for a month of training."

"A whole month?" Her pout deepened.

"Yeah." He suddenly wished it was two months.

"Maybe we can finally grab a coffee when you get back." Her voice was a cheerful neutral, but there was no hiding the hopeful light behind her blue-tinted contacts.

He offered her a two-fingered salute without answering, sincerely hoping she found what she was looking for while he was gone. Despite the divorcee desperation she oozed, she was a nice person who deserved to be happy. He just didn't see himself as the guy to make that happen.

"I'll give a holler when I know for sure what day I'm returning." He backed through the door of his apartment she'd left open, stepping safely out of her reach. "Until then, feel free to throw in some Sunday tours."

"Thanks, Noah." Her voice was soft and wistful. She looked like she wanted to say more, but the elevator doors rolled open behind her, forcing her to twirl around and rejoin her prospective renters.

He shut his front door in relief. *Man!* Leaving the apartment manager's presence always felt a little like dodging a bullet.

He headed straight for his closet to change into a t-shirt, jeans, and cowboy boots. Then he packed nearly all of his meager belongings in the same pair of black suitcases he'd carried into town three years earlier. The only thing on the training center's recommended packing list he was missing was a dog to train with — nothing a quick trip to the nearest animal shelter couldn't fix. He'd never owned a pet before, but how hard could it be to care for a single mutt?

Guess I'm about to find out.

Opting to skip the elevator, he hefted his suitcases down the rear stairwell in lieu of the gym workout he probably wasn't going to get around to today. As he tossed the suitcases inside the quad cab of his silver Dodge Ram, his cell phone vibrated with an incoming call.

A quick glance at the screen verified it was Seven, a buddy of his from his last foster home. Like him, Seven had finally been pulled out of the system by a relative he barely knew, a hard-nosed grandfather. The guy had come to claim Seven the day he retired from the Texas Rangers. He'd been tough on Seven throughout his remaining years of high school, insisting that life would be even tougher on him. As if Seven hadn't already figured that out for himself! Despite his grandfather's unorthodox rearing, Seven had formed enough of a bond with him to follow in his footsteps after high school.

"Hey!" Noah crowed into the mouthpiece, genuinely glad to hear from him. "How are the Rangers treating you?"

"Like a king with the usual long hours and low pay." Seven chuckled, not sounding the least bit perturbed by those dismal facts. "How's the force treating you?"

"Same as the Rangers are treating you. Did you get my text?"

"That's why I'm calling."

"No kidding!" He'd been a little hesitant to inform Seven about his acceptance into Texas Hotline Training Center, since they'd both applied at the same time.

"According to our packing list, you're going to need a dog to train with."

It took an extra second for Noah's brain to digest the full import of Seven's words. When he did, he was unable to contain his war whoop of elation, which made a woman walking past his truck jolt in alarm.

Sorry! He mouthed a quick apology to her before shouting into the phone, "You made it in!" It was incredible news.

"Yep." The lack of elation in Seven's voice threw up the first red flag of alarm in Noah's gut.

"You don't sound too excited. What's going on?"

"So, ah...my wife just filed for a separation."

What? Noah felt sick all the way to his gut. It was the last thing he'd been expecting his friend to say. "I'm sorry to hear it." *Man, I sound lame!* But he didn't know what else to say.

"You and me both, brother." Seven's voice grew suspiciously hoarse.

"Is it something you care to talk about?" Noah felt obligated to make the offer, though he wasn't all that sure what the difference was between a separation and a divorce. And he sure as heck was no poster boy when it came to relationships.

"Nope."

Whew! "I'm really sorry, man." It certainly explained his friend's lack of excitement about his acceptance into the training center.

"Back to the reason for my call." There was a tortured note to Seven's voice that made Noah want to punch something. The guy had seriously suffered enough in his life, and now this.

Come on, God! Where are you, Big Guy?

"Listening," he muttered into the mouthpiece.

"The skinny of it is this. I gotta police dog I need you take off my hands."

"Whoa! Seriously?" The timing couldn't have been more perfect. Maybe he wouldn't have to squeeze in a detour to the animal shelter, after all.

"Yeah. She's a Rottweiler named Java, who served with a search and rescue unit in Dallas for a little over five years."

"Wait a sec," Noah interrupted. As much as he appreciated Seven thinking of him, it made no sense for him to pass up owning a police dog for himself. "Why aren't you taking her?"

"Because I'm gonna be tied up with legal garbage for the next couple of months."

His words served as an icy punch to Noah's gut. "Please tell me your separation with Tiff isn't knocking you out of the training altogether."

"It's not. I just confirmed it with the Admissions Office today. They're gonna let me roll my attendance forward a few months. You know...let the dust settle first."

"I see." It twisted Noah's gut all over again to realize how close they'd come to being classmates. And now they weren't going to be.

"So, do you want the dog or not?" Seven demanded impatiently

"Of course I want the dog!" Noah exploded. "I just..." It didn't feel right celebrating his good fortune at his friend's expense. "Yes," he added in a quieter voice. "I want the dog. I'll take good care of her for you until—"

"She's yours, man," Seven cut in. "No strings attached. Once you train with her, you'll form a bond. That's how this works."

"What are you going to do for a dog, then?"

"The search and rescue team that's giving her up is a group of volunteers that's disbanding. I already have dibs on one of the other dogs they're re-homing."

"Okay." That made Noah feel a little better, though he was still plenty sick at heart about Seven and Tiffany's pending separation. "When can we meet?"

"How about this afternoon?" Seven gave a mirthless laugh. "I assume you'll be heading in my direction soon?"

"Actually, I was just about to get on the road."

"Figured that."

———

THE MOMENT FARRAH CARMICHAEL ended her phone call, she gave a shriek of sheer excitement. "Omigosh! Omigosh! Omigosh!" She danced around the tiny kitchen of the cottage she shared with her mother on the outskirts of Dallas. "I got selected, Mom!" She'd landed one of the highly coveted dog handler internships at the world-renowned Texas Hotline Training Center. Her dog grooming days were over. She was moving up to the big leagues.

Her impromptu celebration ended in an oomph of pain as she bumped into the rounded butcher block corner of the preparation island her mother had insisted on installing a few weeks earlier. *Ouch!* Farrah rubbed a hand over her hip. That was going to leave a bruise. She was never going to get used to having a cabinet right smack in the middle of their kitchen.

She was surprised when none of her noise-making brought her mother running. Though she worked nights, vacuuming and scrubbing office buildings all over town with her Bloom Where You're Planted cleaning service, Nancy Carmichael was usually out of bed by the dinner hour. It was their daily dose of mother-daughter time.

"Mom?" Still rubbing her hip, Farrah half-jogged and half-limped her way down the short hallway to her mother's bedroom at the back of the house. The door was propped open enough to see that her mother was no longer in bed.

"Mom?" Farrah called again, glancing over her shoulder toward the living room. There was no glow from a television and no sounds coming from that direction. The first tendrils of alarm curled through her midsection. "Mom, are you home?"

"Yes."

The weak tenor of her mother's voice had Farrah lurching through the bedroom door and glancing wildly around the room. The cane chair that was normally pushed beneath her mother's sewing desk was lying on its side in the middle of the room beneath the ceiling fan. It looked like someone had been standing on it to change a lightbulb.

Oh, no! Farrah's hand flew to her chest. "Where are you, Mom?"

"In here, baby."

She followed her voice into the small adjoining bathroom and found her mother perched on the toilet seat with her slender arms wrapped around her middle. The third member of their small family, Snitch, was lying at her feet. His saggy cocker spaniel features were infused with concern. At the sight of Farrah, he gave a small yip of welcome, but didn't budge from his vigil over her mother.

"Are you sick?" Farrah's gaze dropped to the tub of water her mother had her foot resting in. "You're hurt!" She slid to her knees and reached hesitantly for her mother's swollen ankle that she was soaking in the cold tap water.

Snitch made a whining sound, as if begging Farrah not to jostle the injured limb any more than necessary.

She smoothed a hand reassuringly over his silky blonde head as she murmured, "It looks..."

"Fractured, I know," her mother sighed. She was a petite woman who'd always managed to look half her age. Her jeans were fashionably frayed at the knees — from genuine wear and tear, in her case — and her shoulder-length hair was twisted into a careless ponytail, a perfect honey-brown hue that came out of the same bottle of dye that Farrah's did. They were often mistaken for sisters.

"Why aren't you at the hospital?" Farrah demanded.

Nancy Carmichael shook her head in regret. "Baby, you know we can't afford to get stuck with a big fat ambulance bill. Not to mention—"

"I'll take you." Farrah's brain raced feverishly.

She had a little over fifteen hundred dollars saved up. It was probably enough to cover a trip to the urgent care center with all the co-pays it would entail. Her mother was going to need an x-ray, a cast, and probably a prescription for some pain pills.

"No need," her mother assured gently. "Dr. Evans has already agreed to stop by here on his way home from work."

His office was one of the buildings her mother cleaned every weekend.

"Mom, this isn't the time to call in a favor for a quickie home visit," Farrah protested. "You need real medical attention." *Good gracious!* What was the point of them having medical insurance when her mother always refused to use it?

"He's bringing his nurse with a plaster kit and everything. I already sent him pictures, and he already assured me it's no more than a simple fracture."

Farrah couldn't believe how nonchalant her mother was acting about the whole thing. Her ankle was broken, for crying out loud! "But—"

"No buts, baby." Nancy Carmichael forced a smile to her pale lips. "Now tell me. What were you carrying on so loud about in the kitchen a few minutes ago?"

"What?" Farrah blinked at her. "Oh." Her heart sank. "I got a call from the admissions department at the Texas Hotline Training Center."

Her mother's expression brightened. "You got accepted?" A smile brightened her pale features. "Oh, baby, I knew you would!" As she reached over to squeeze her daughter's hand, Snitch gave an excited yip.

Her fingers felt so cold that Farrah stared at her in dismay. "I'm not going." How could she? "There's no way I'm leaving you alone like this."

"Of course you're going!" her mother snapped. "You've been applying for that blasted internship for two straight years."

"I don't see how." Farrah wiped her damp fingers on her jeans, leaving two dark hand prints on the denim. *You can't drive. You can't work.* "Who will cover your night shift?" The training center was a sizable campus, which her mother just so happened to be under contract to clean five nights per week. Farrah had ridden along countless times in her mother's van to help out. Mopping her way past the big bulletin board outside the Admissions Office was how she'd found out about the summer internship opportunity.

"Lavina says she can work for me from midnight until six for the next eight weeks, give or take a few days."

Farrah nodded, unsurprised to learn that Lavina had already offered to help. She was her mother's best friend. "Who's going to cover for you from ten to midnight?"

Her mother grimaced. "Actually, I was kind of hoping *you* would." She hastened to add, "I know it's not ideal with you starting your internship and all, but at least you'll already be there at the campus." She spread her hands. "Can't get a much shorter commute than that, huh?"

"I, ah..." Farrah struggled to wrap her brain around the notion of interning during the day and cleaning a few hours each evening. "We might be able to make it work." It would cut heavily into her study time, of course, and it would all but eliminate her chances of hanging out with any of those hunky law enforcement students after hours. *Bummer!*

"It *will* work," her mother corrected firmly. "It has to. We Carmichael women are accustomed to making do." It was one of her favorite expressions. Having been widowed over twenty years, she was the queen of making do.

"You're right, Mom." The tension in Farrah's shoulders eased. "We're going to get through this." Now that the decision had been made, excitement flooded her all over again. *Holy smokes!* Feeling a little overcome, she bent forward to wrap her arms around Snitch's neck and received a sloppy kiss in return. *I'm about to become the intern of a world-famous dog handler at the blasted Texas Hotline Training Center!*

While also serving as a lowly maid inside those same hallowed hallways...

She gave a breathy laugh against the top of Snitch's head. Life sure had its curve balls. At least the maid stuff would only be temporary. The internship, on the other hand, was going to open doors she'd hardly dared to even dream about until now.

CHAPTER 2: ACCIDENTAL ENCOUNTERS

FARRAH

Farrah hated the necessity of driving her mother's commercial van to the Texas Hotline Training Center. *Seriously, peeps!* What single, twenty-five-year-old female wanted to show up at the coolest campus on the planet in a white, window-less van with a bright pink, orange, and green company logo splashed across both sides? Especially one depicting an enormous cartoon flower in an enormous cartoon flowerpot. *Ugh!*

The name of her mother's company was sort of a private joke between them. Bloom Where You're Planted was actually the name of her mother's first attempt at running her own business, a mobile florist that had failed miserably during the first six months. Instead of coming up with a whole new name for her next entrepreneurial venture, which would've required purchasing new business cards and a bazillion other supplies, she had simply started her cleaning service under the same name. This time, it had taken off.

They weren't wealthy, by any means, but their small home was paid for, and they had no debts. Farrah had been making noises about moving out and getting her own place, but her mother kept insisting that she "wait until the time was right."

Today, more than ever before, Farrah felt like she was getting closer to the right time for a lot of things. She gripped the steering wheel tighter as she turned into the parking lot of the training center's main auditorium. *Here I am.* Butterflies filled her stomach at the realization that her coming and going from the center would no longer be restricted to service entrances and rear exits. This time, she would be marching right through the front doors.

As she found a parking spot, an unexpected wave of pride rolled through her. She wasn't wealthy, didn't come from a big family name, and had no VIP references to cushion the screening process. She'd truly earned this. Hopping down from the driver's seat, she looped her crossbody purse over her head and jogged around to the rear of the van. An April breeze wafted across the parking lot, stirring the fumes of freshly sealed asphalt.

Farrah gave the air a tentative sniff. To her, it was the scent of progress. Throwing the van's rear double doors wide, she reached for the handle of her roller suitcase.

"Excuse me, ma'am." The husky male voice made her spin around.

She found herself facing a tall cowboy in tinted aviator glasses. His dark hair was clipped short on the sides, and he was sporting a fresh shave. The sharp angle of his jaw and hard line of his mouth practically shouted he was a cop.

"Hey." She smiled curiously at him. "Were you talking to me?"

"I was if you work here, ma'am."

Ma'am? She swallowed a chuckle while arching her eyebrows at him. There was no way he was younger than her. If she had to guess, she'd peg him for closer to thirty than twenty. "I sure do. Who's asking?"

"Police Detective Noah Zeller." He straightened to his full height, which made him tower over her much shorter five-foot-four frame. "I'm a student here. About to be, anyway." Glancing away, he lifted his Stetson to run a hand through his short hair. "Sorry to barrel over here like this, but my dog is sick and—"

"Where is he?" she interrupted sharply.

"It's a she. Her name is Java." He angled his head toward a silver pickup that was parked only a few spots down from her mother's van. "I'm her new owner and...never mind. It's a long story."

One that apparently wasn't worth repeating to just any old stranger in a parking lot. Farrah stiffened at his dismissive tone. "I'll take a look at her." His dog didn't deserve to suffer just because her owner was a bit of a stuffed shirt.

He grimaced. "Actually, ma'am, I was only hoping to borrow some paper towels." He gestured at her mother's van.

I see. Her smile slipped. *You merely require the services of a cleaning lady.* Without another word, she mechanically reached for a roll of paper towels and a bottle of disinfectant spray. So much for her hopes of meeting a few swoony guys in uniform this summer. This one apparently couldn't see past the commercial decal on her mother's van. During their short encounter, he'd yet to look directly at her.

She was about to hand the cleaning supplies to him when a wicked thought struck her. "I bet cleaning is more my specialty than yours. How about you show me the mess your dog made and let me take care of it for you?"

He looked surprised. "You don't have to do that, ma'am. She ah...threw up in the bed of my truck. It's not a campus vehicle."

"True, but you're currently parked on campus, so I'm willing to make an exception," she returned, trying not to laugh. "Do you want my help or not, detective?" She playfully brandished her spray bottle in the air.

"If you truly don't mind, ma'am." Looking relieved, he motioned for her to follow him the short distance to his truck. "I really appreciate this, Miss, er..." He paused. "I don't believe I caught your name."

She waved at her mother's van. "Bloom," she lied. "The maid." Unfortunately, that last part was true. "We're the training center's cleaning service."

"Nice to meet you, Bloom," he intoned politely.

Her lips twitched, but she sobered the moment she glanced into the bed of his truck. A lovely chocolate Rottweiler was lying there with her head resting glumly on her paws. The contents of her stomach were piled beside her.

Farrah was relieved to see it was nothing more than the dog food she'd most recently eaten. "Oh, you poor thing," she murmured sympathetically. To Noah Zeller, she demanded, "When did you last feed her?"

He frowned. "I don't know. A few hours ago, maybe."

She pointed at the mess. "This looks more recent."

"I have no idea when she ate. It was a three-and-a-half hour drive."

She was aghast. "You mean you left her food bowl inside her cage?"

"Yep. Didn't know when she'd get hungry."

Well, that explains a lot. It looked to Farrah like a

simple case of overeating. "She's a search and rescue dog. They're accustomed to structure." *Good golly!* Those were the ABCs of dog handling. How could he not know this? "That usually includes a feeding schedule." Shaking her head, she quickly cleaned up the mess and disinfected the area. Marching a few yards away, she deposited the soiled paper towels in a trashcan.

"I'm new at this," he called after her, "in case you missed that part."

"Clearly," she shot back. "What kind of food are you giving her?"

"How about I just show you?" Sounding sheepish, he picked up a white plastic cylindrical container and popped off the lid.

The round little pellets looked alright at first glance. However, there was only one way to be sure. Picking up a single kernel of dog food, Farrah popped it into her mouth. She chewed a moment, then spit it out. "Gross!" Lifting her angry gaze to his, she was amazed to find him gaping at her with something akin to horror.

"Did you seriously just—?"

"It's stale," she interrupted coolly. "No wonder the poor thing gave it back to you." She pointed at his dog. "She's not sick. She's mostly pouting over her sub-par menu options. Haven't you ever seen a female pout?"

A shadow crossed his face. "It's what the last

owner gave me when I adopted her," he explained, sounding exasperated.

"If it was me, I'd throw it out. All of it." Farrah knew she was being merciless, but his instructors were going to be far tougher on him when he started his official training tomorrow. Glancing down at her watch, she muttered, "You've got time to resupply with fresh stuff. If I were you, I'd do it. You're going to need Java in tip-top shape in the morning." He was also going to need the dog on his side. If he planned on successfully completing his training, the two of them would need to form an air-tight partnership in the coming days.

The police detective studied Farrah for a moment. When he finally started speaking again, it was in a grudging voice. "You seem to know a lot about dogs."

She smiled tightly. "Can't say the same for you, officer." She had a niggling feeling that the guy was going to crash and burn in the morning. She almost felt sorry for him.

"Got it," he retorted dryly. Leaning back against the open door of his truck bed, he idly scratched Java behind the ears. She made a growling sound in the back of her throat, but it was a soft growl — almost like a purr. "It's Noah, by the way."

"What?" Farrah's gaze jerked back to his.

"My name is Noah, Bloom. Surely, wading

through dog vomit together qualifies us to be on a first-name basis."

His comment surprised her. Maybe she'd been a little too quick to pass judgement on him. "You sure you want to be on a first-name basis with a maid who eats dog food?" she inquired sweetly.

"Yeah." The lack of hesitation in his response sent a small thrill of excitement through her. "You already steered me out of my first calamity. Who knows when I'll need you to come to my rescue again."

A chuckle escaped her. "Good point. A lady armed to the teeth with mops, brooms, and disinfectant spray could prove to be a useful ally."

"My thoughts exactly." For this first time during their encounter, he grinned.

It transformed the hard angles of his features into a cowboy heartthrob that made her knees go weak. *Whoa, buddy! You could have at least warned me.* She struggled to collect her scattered emotions.

"Any final words of advice for me?" He waggled his brows at her.

"I, ah..." She was having trouble processing what he'd said. She was too busy melting beneath the blinding wattage of his smile.

"What all should I buy at the pet store?" He folded his arms, which were so corded with muscle that she had to wonder if he was showing them off for her benefit. "Should I just grab one of everything in the dog food aisle?"

He was downright lady killer material — way out of her league, unfortunately. She was more into blue jeans and dog slobber. The thought was enough to help her regain control of her senses. "You don't have time for experiments. I'd just load up on some high-quality food for an adult dog. High on protein and other nutrients. Be sure to check the expiration date."

He nodded. "Anything else?"

Her normal supply of devilry returned. "Yeah. Stock up on milk bones. Since the two of you are new partners, you're going to need to win her over quickly." The center's instructors would square him away on how, when, and why to use them as rewards during training. "Oh, and lose the ratty collar." Java's collar had seen better days. It might've once been blue, but it was too faded and stained to say for sure. "Get her something with a little pep in it, like red or pink."

"Will do." He nodded. "Thanks."

"No problem." She took a step back. Her little tete-a-tete in the parking lot with Noah Zeller was making her cut it close to the start time of her in-processing appointment in Human Resources. "I ah...better get going. They're expecting me inside." She was careful to avoid saying who was expecting her.

"I'll see you around." He gave her a lazy two-fingered salute that, for some inexplicable reason, melted her heart all over again.

Get a grip, woman! She pivoted and started walking back to her mother's van.

"Hey, wait a sec."

Can't. I'm out of time. She glanced over her shoulder, but didn't stop walking.

"You never told me your last name."

I sure didn't. Hiding a smile, she opted for the truth this time. "It's Carmichael." As she reached for the handle of her suitcase, she could feel his gaze on her. Not good if she hoped to maintain her ruse as Bloom, the maid. With a silent sigh, she dropped her arm and left her suitcase in the back of the van. She could come back for it later. Instead, she hooked the straps of her backpack over one shoulder and slammed the doors shut.

Sensing that Noah was still watching her, she fluttered a hand in the air and headed for the front doors of the main building.

———

I'M STARING *at her like an idiot.* Noah didn't know why it was so hard to look away from Bloom Carmichael. Maybe it was because he was single and lonely. It had been over a year since his last date. Yep, he was definitely in a dry spell.

Which still didn't explain how the cleaning woman had managed to utterly fascinate him during their short encounter. She wasn't his usual type and couldn't have been more different from his ex. Celina was all designer clothing, manicures, and expensive perfume — with overtones of feminine helplessness that drew men like bees to nectar. In comparison, Bloom was a statement of self-reliance. After a single conversation with her, he had no doubt that the spitfire in blue jeans and a ponytail could handle anything that life threw her way.

She practically oozed confidence, a trait he found a bit surprising for someone who wielded a mop and broom for a living. Then again, she'd managed to land a cleaning contract with the renowned Texas Hotline Training Center. That took some real negotiating skills. There was definitely more to the petite maid than met the eye. She might not be an ounce over a hundred pounds sopping wet, but every inch of her was as feisty as all get out. He sincerely hoped he got to see her again soon.

For reasons that made no sense to him, his brain leaped ahead to a scenario in which he returned to Houston with the smoking hot maid for a girlfriend. Boy, wouldn't that give the stodgy social elite something new to chew on? It was never going to happen, of course. The best possible outcome of his month-long stay at the training center was the successful completion of their Urban Rescue Training Program.

As of tomorrow morning, there would be no more time for flirting with Bloom, much less dating her.

As he returned Java to her cage, he noticed a pink cleaning cloth lying next to it. Figuring it belonged to Bloom, he grabbed one of the specimen bags he kept around and stuffed it inside. Hopefully, he'd be able to return it to her soon.

Then he stooped to bring himself eye level with Java. "Sorry about the stale food, partner. You and I are going to rectify that matter right away." He left the door of his truck bed down long enough for her to watch him march the canister of expired dog food to the trash can. He pulled off the lid and dumped its contents.

The Rottweiler gave two shrill barks, making him wonder if she understood every word he'd said. He returned her cage to his air-conditioned cab and drove with her to the nearest pet store he could locate on his GPS.

Since Bloom had assured him Java wasn't truly ill, he felt safe putting her in her harness and bringing her inside the store with him. The dog started prancing around excitedly the moment her paws hit the pavement. No doubt she was glad to finally be out of her cage.

"Come on, girl." He gave a low whistle to get her moving toward the front entrance. "Let's go shopping."

He walked her up and down every aisle that

contained doggy supplies, filling his cart with dog food, milk bones, a new cushion for her to sleep on inside her cage, and the new collar Bloom had suggested he purchase. After a short deliberation, he picked out the brightest pink one on the rack. Pulling off the price tag, he took a knee beside Java and proceeded to swap out her old one for the new one right away.

She held still while he did the honors, wagging her tail so wildly it was a wonder she didn't wag it right off. *Shoot!* He might not know jack about taking care of dogs, but Bloom was right about one thing. Java strutted to the checkout counter as if she was very much aware that she was sporting a new collar.

While he waited in line, he eyed the racks of quick-grab items on either side of them. To his amazement, Java pushed her muzzle right up to a package containing a pair of blue rubber balls.

"You want to play ball, eh?" An undeniable baseball nut, he didn't mind that fact one bit.

She made a whining sound in the back of her throat and sniffed the balls again.

Wondering if her last owner had taught her to play fetch, Noah grabbed a package of the balls and added them to his cart. He wasn't sure if there'd be any time at the training center for tossing around balls, but it wouldn't hurt to be prepared.

"I think she's enjoying your shopping spree."

The kind, motherly voice made Noah glance up at the woman in line behind them.

"Uh, thanks." He couldn't think of anything else to say. He was too busy experiencing the sensation of being sucker punched in the gut. The woman was a dead ringer for Bloom Carmichael — an older version, of course. Still, she had the same brown hair pulled up in the same sassy ponytail. Her slender frame was clad in a similar pair of frayed jeans, with one big exception. Hers were rolled at the ankle on one side to reveal a thick white cast. She was leaning on a pair of crutches with a dog leash looped around one of the handles.

A cocker spaniel stood motionless beside her. He studied Noah with an age-old expression that made him wonder if the creature could tell he had absolutely no idea what he was doing as a dog owner.

Java growled low in her throat, and Noah snapped his fingers at her. "That's enough!" He glanced back over at the petite woman on crutches. "Sorry about that. I'm a new dog owner." He hoped that explained why his dog was being so rude to her dog.

The woman glanced merrily at the contents of his cart. "I think you're starting off on the right foot," she assured.

"I wish that was the case," he sighed. "Turns out the food bucket that was handed down to me had expired. Gave her an upset stomach. This is me, scrambling to make it up to her before we begin our training together in the morning."

The woman's brown eyes sharpened with interest. "Does that mean you're a student at the Texas Hotline Training Center?"

"Sure does, ma'am." He tipped the brim of his Stetson at her. "I met a woman there about a half hour ago who could pass for your twin. Does the name Bloom Carmichael ring a bell?"

She blinked her long, dark lashes in surprise. "As a matter of fact, she's my daughter," she announced proudly.

That figures.

"What did you do to make her mad?" the woman asked curiously.

It was Noah's turn to blink. "How did you know I made her mad?"

"Her name is Farrah. The only time she introduces herself as Bloom is when she's really annoyed."

His face burned with embarrassment. "I don't think she was overly impressed with my dog handling skills. She advised me in no uncertain terms to invest in some new supplies immediately."

"That sounds like her." Mrs. Carmichael chuckled. "I'm Nancy Carmichael, by the way, the wounded owner of Bloom Where You're Planted." She gestured ruefully down at her crutches. "Broke my ankle. That's the only reason Farrah is stuck covering for me at the training center."

So Farrah wasn't truly a maid, after all? Or was she? Noah was more intrigued than ever by the sharp-tongued, snapping-eyed beauty and her mother. "Sorry about your ankle, ma'am."

She shrugged. "I can only blame myself. Instead of standing on a chair, I should've taken the time to fetch a ladder."

"Ouch!" He grimaced in sympathy, unable to fault her open-faced honesty. A lot of folks weren't half as good at owning up to their mistakes.

"Eh, enough about my stupidity." She waved a hand in derision. "What are you at the training center for?"

"Urban Rescue." He didn't bother going into any detail about it. Since she worked at the center, she was probably already familiar with their programs.

She nodded, making no effort to hide her admiration. "You're in for some real fun, Mr. ah..."

"Police Detective Noah Zeller. I'm off the clock right now, so just call me Noah." Glancing down at her crutches, he added, "I'd offer to shake your hand, but..."

She smiled warmly at him, making the corners of her eyes crinkle. "I wish you the very best in your training, Noah."

Her motherly tone went straight to the loneliest corner of his chest and settled there. "Thanks, ma'am." It was the first real congratulations he'd received. The police chief had mainly crabbed about

Noah's forthcoming absence from the department, and Seven had been too caught up in his personal misery over his and Tiff's pending separation to offer much in the way of well wishes.

"Nancy," she corrected gently. "I happen to be off duty for the next six or eight weeks, myself, so it's just Nancy."

They chatted amicably the rest of the time they were in line together. Noah ended up carrying her purchases to her car, where he met Lavina, a woman she introduced as her best friend. Lavina was a typical, has-been diva, probably a cheerleader back in her high school days. She wore too much makeup, her hands were heavily calloused, and her skin was tanned to the consistency of shoe leather. Her conversation was far more countrified than Nancy and Farrah's, her mannerisms far less refined.

She made the Carmichaels seem downright classy in comparison, despite their jeans. More educated. The mother-daughter team didn't fit the typical cleaning staff profile, that's for sure. His extra detective senses were telling him that the two of them were something more. Something special.

CHAPTER 3: FIRST DAY SURPRISES
NOAH

Noah drove back to the training center, feeling strangely fortunate to have met the Carmichaels. He liked them, which was more than he could say for most people he met. While in foster care, he'd honed and polished his gift of suspicion. Trust didn't come easily for him. He was still trying to figure out why he'd wasted a drop of it on Celina Manning, though he could probably chalk it up to a weak moment. Or loneliness. Or the desire to meet Mrs. Right some day.

When his brain was firing on all pistons, however, he questioned everyone and everything around him. It was probably what made him a good detective. At the moment, he was pondering the odds of meeting a woman who shared the same first name as the heiress in his missing persons case. Farrah wasn't exactly a common name. Yet here he was, searching for a woman named Farrah Carstens while enjoying a chance encounter with a woman named Farrah Carmichael.

It didn't feel like a mere coincidence — more like fate.

Unfortunately, he hadn't made that stellar of a first impression on her. Quite the opposite. She'd gone out of her way to make him feel like a dunce, not that he blamed her. He *was* a dunce when it came to dog ownership. He'd never owned a pet before. Considering that he would be starting his Urban Rescue training in the morning, he hoped his learning curve would be mercifully short.

Despite his lack of expertise in doggy care, he was looking forward to his training. He was also hoping like crazy that his path would cross with that of a certain feisty maid again.

By the time he arrived back on campus, a whole team of training center personnel was stationed beneath a row of blue and white canopy tents on the main sidewalk. They checked his ID, verified his paperwork, and assigned him a dorm room. Then they pointed him toward the dog kennel, advising him to get Java settled in first.

He returned to his truck and drove to the kennel with his small mountain of dog food and other supplies. The kennel was a chaotic blur of dog owners chatting with attendants, barking dogs, sharp commands, whistles, and the sounds of metal cage doors clanging open and shut.

A tall, energetic figure in black cargo pants and shiny black combat boots sauntered up to him. Her reddish-blonde hair was pulled back in a severe bun beneath a black service cap that was pulled too low for him to read her expression. However, there was something vaguely familiar about her.

"It's a bit of a mad house in here this evening, isn't it?" Looking amused, she surveyed the students scrambling to get their dogs housed in their assigned cages.

He wasn't sure why one of the instructors had singled him out for a conversation, but he straightened and answered in his most respectful voice, "Couldn't have said it better myself, ma'am." He scanned the laminated name tags hanging from the metal cages closest to him. Java's name wasn't on any of them.

"Captain Alicia Downs." The woman thrust a hand in his direction.

He gaped at her tanned fingers for a moment. No wonder she looked so familiar. She was the training center's celebrity dog handler instructor, a retired Army officer with many deployments under her belt. He'd read about her heroism on the battlefield, tracking down American hostages with the help of her canine partner. She'd also successfully routed out pockets of enemy combatants, thereby thwarting major ambushes on her troops.

Feeling like he'd won the lottery, Noah shook her hand. "I'm Police Detective Noah Zeller, ma'am. It's such an honor to meet you." *Wow!* She was a walking, talking legend in combat boots.

She angled her head at Java, who was perched on her haunches at his side. "How long have you and your lovely lady been together?"

His heart sank at the realization that their conversation was quickly deteriorating into confession time. "Less than twenty-four hours."

She pursed her lips. "That's a bold move, attending a rigorous training program like this with a new partner in crime at your side."

The skepticism in her voice wasn't lost on him. "She has over five years of search and rescue experience."

"What about you?"

"Seven years, ma'am. My department specializes in missing persons cases." Not wanting to misrepresent his expertise, he quickly added, "In the past, we've depended on various search and rescue units in Houston. Considering how vital the first twenty-four hours are in a missing persons case, our chief decided that's not good enough. Going forward, his goal is for every detective on our team to become SAR qualified." Noah was the first Guinea pig.

She sobered. "You mean you're new to dog

handling?" She didn't make it sound like a good thing.

"I'm new to dog ownership. Period." His foster family hadn't been able to afford any extra mouths to feed. His great-uncle had been too feeble on his cane to risk bringing a live, furry tripping hazard into the house. And Noah had always worked such long hours, he didn't feel right acquiring a pet he wouldn't be around to enjoy, much less care for.

The captain's mouth tightened as she glanced down at her watch. "You do realize we have less than twelve hours before show time, detective?"

"Yes, ma'am." How could he forget?

"You should spend every second of those twelve hours getting your dog acclimated."

"Acclimated, ma'am?" He understood the dictionary definition of the word, but he sensed there was more to her point than that.

"Yes, acclimated," she snapped. "To you, your voice, and your commands. You may have acquired a dog with cutting edge skills, but they won't be worth squat if you're not in full command of them, come tomorrow morning."

"How do you suggest I do that, ma'am?" He could really use a few pointers.

"Train." There was a note of finality in her voice. "Now. This evening. All night if you have to. Train like someone's life depends upon it." Her gaze glinted with fiery conviction. "Because some day, it will."

"Thank you, ma'am." He inclined his head respectfully. "I will."

The hint of a twinkle worked its way through the ferocity of her gaze. "I'm sure the proof will be in the pudding, as the old saying goes." He knew she meant that there would be no hiding his progress, or lack thereof, during tomorrow's class session.

"You won't be disappointed, ma'am." He wasn't bragging. He was making her a promise.

With one last measuring look, the captain moved on down the line to greet other incoming students.

Noah whistled at Java to start moving again. Her lithe brown body wiggled with excitement as they passed a trio of perfectly behaved dogs. She yipped at each one of them, earning Noah a whole range of looks from their owners — everything from pity to disdain.

"Nice tail you got there on your lapdog," one of them noted in a snide voice.

He nodded to acknowledge his words, without responding or pausing to introduce himself. He knew the guy was referring to the fact that his Rottweiler didn't have a docked tail like many police dogs did, and no wonder. She'd been raised by a group of volunteers — not hard core men in uniform like themselves.

Noah noted how his fellow classmates' dogs

remained sitting quietly on their haunches as he and Java passed by them. *Looks like I brought the happiest mutt to the party.*

Yeah, he got the fact that most of his classmates were already far more skilled at dog handling than he was. *Big whoop!* He'd never been overly impressed by degrees and certifications. At the end of the day, the only thing that mattered was solving cases, finding missing people, and bringing them safely home. If his search and rescue dog did it with a bit of swagger, so be it. There was no way Seven would have talked him into adopting a dog that wasn't up to the task. The captain was right, though. Noah and Java needed to take their new partnership on a test drive as soon as possible.

He finally located her assigned cage and was pleased to see the key was resting in the lock. After depositing her inside, he first filled her water bowl. He was about to fill her food bowl, but he remembered Farrah's warning about search and rescue dogs being accustomed to more discipline.

"Sit," he ordered firmly.

Without hesitation, Java plopped down on her furry backside.

He was impressed to note all her wiggling and jiggling had ceased. It was like a switch had been turned off. She went from playful to all-business in a heartbeat, watching him expectantly.

Relief coursed through him. *Alright, then. Let's*

do this! If he took her outside to train for the next half hour, it would put her dinner time at the crack of six. *Sounds like a decent enough feeding schedule to me.* He filled both of his pockets with her doggy treats and opened the door to her cage.

On their way out of the kennel, Noah reviewed the basics with Java. He sat her next to him, then ordered her to heel. She obediently fell into step beside him. To his amusement, they passed by the same three dogs, whose owners were still chatting and sizing up the competition. At least, that's what it felt like. He ignored them. This wasn't summer camp. They weren't required to be friends.

According to the Texas Hotline Training Center's published stats, only about 65-70% of the students graduated the first time around. That meant about a third of his classmates would either wash out or get recycled into the next class. He fully intended to be among those who graduated.

Once outside, he jogged with Java to a distant field, hoping to achieve some modicum of privacy. He found an enclosed grassy area. Since the gate was open, he figured it was okay to enter.

Java gave an excited yip, but otherwise remained at his side.

"Sit," Noah ordered again.

She sat.

"Good girl." He held out a doggy treat and allowed her to eat it out of his hand. "Stay," he said next, showing her his open palm as he backed away from her.

She watched him without moving.

He increased his stride, still walking backwards, and finally broke into a backwards jog.

She never took her eyes off of him.

He stopped and waited a second. Then he beckoned to her. "Come, Java!"

She bolted with energy in his direction.

Instead of making her stop and sit this time, he held out his arms to her. She leaped into them, sending them tumbling to the ground together.

He chuckled as she licked his chin. "You're something else, Java." She nosed at his pockets as he scratched her behind her ears. He obligingly gave her another treat. He didn't care how many of his classmates stared down their noses at his methods. As far as he was concerned, he and Java were off to a good start.

He saw no reason to veer from the basics this evening. She was already highly trained. Instead, he focused on building rapport. He wrapped up their first training session with a good old fashioned game of fetch.

Java was ecstatic when he produced one of the blue balls. He waved it in the air a few times to build her anticipation before giving it a hearty toss. She bounded after it, barking like it was a live rabbit. Then she dashed madly in his direction with it clenched between her jaws. Instead of dropping it at his feet, she tipped her head up to him and waited for him to extend a hand to her. She dropped it neatly in his palm.

"Very good, Java!" As a reward, he threw the ball again and again and again. Only when they ran out of time did he pocket it and give her a final milk bone.

"Time for dinner, girl." He waited until she was standing beside him again before commanding her to heel.

They walked side-by-side back to the kennel.

Though Captain Downs had made it sound like Noah should spend every last second of his evening with Java, he headed back to his truck to retrieve his suitcases. With all due respect, this wasn't a battlefield in Afghanistan. If he was going to successfully pass the Urban Rescue Training Program, he needed to take care of himself, too.

Rolling his suitcases to the male dorm, he found himself inside a long, narrow room lined with bunk beds on both sides. *Great.* With this many men sleeping in the same room, it would probably require earplugs to block out all the snoring. Fortunately, he kept a set in the drawer of his dashboard for trips to the shooting range. He would swing by the truck after dinner to grab them.

He swiftly unloaded the contents of his suitcase into the storage trunk at the base of his bed and secured it with the combination lock they'd given him during check-in. By the time he made his way to the cafeteria, it was less than twenty minutes before the closing time posted on the door.

Fortunately, the food line was short. There were only two other students in front of him. Noah grabbed a tray from the cart at the front of the line and selected a set of silverware from a trio of metal canisters. The cafeteria line was eerily reminiscent of his high school days back in Houston, right down to the compartmentalized plastic trays.

"Man! This brings back memories!" A broad-shouldered man with dark skin swooped into line behind Noah, leaning in to chuckle in his ear. "Think we can sweet talk the lunch ladies into serving seconds to us football players?" He mimed throwing a ball across the room.

Nice guess. Noah wasn't sure how the guy had figured out he used to be a quarterback, but that was cool. Due to his clowning around, Noah was pretty sure he hadn't noticed the change of guard taking place in front of them.

He cleared his throat suggestively, trying to draw his attention to the older fella in an apron, who was now standing on the other side of the glass. He held a spatula and was sporting a sneer.

"I'm Vance, by the way." The former football player thrust out a large paw to Noah. "Vance Briggs. Dallas PD, since I didn't make the cut for the NFL.

Poor Cowboys have no idea what they missed out on." He winked.

Noah shook his hand, grinning. "Noah Zeller, Houston PD. Didn't attract too many scouts myself." There had been no time and money for the extra training and conditioning it would've required, but that was okay with him. In his experience, things had a way of working out the way they were meant to be.

"The Cowboys aren't the ones who are about to miss out," the lunch attendant growled. "The food line is closing in fifteen minutes."

The surprise on Vance's face indicated he was noticing the man for the first time. "Hey! Didn't see you come in." He peered past the attendant's shoulder, as if trying to figure out where the lunch lady had gone.

"Clearly." The cafeteria attendant folded his burly, tattooed arms. It made the fabric beneath his name tag bunch up. It read, *Bill*. "If you're still planning on sweet-talking me into those seconds, I'm all ears."

Vance made a choking sound that he attempted to cover with a cough. Smirking, he pointed at the man's hands with a comical flourish. "Those are some nice rubber gloves you have on, sir. Think I heard somewhere that silicon blue is the new pink."

Bill's upper lip curled. "Ain't never heard that one before."

"It's true," Vance insisted in an innocent voice,

waggling his eyebrows at Noah. His expression was a plea for backup.

Keeping a straight face, Noah nodded. "Yeah, I heard that somewhere, too." He held a hand over his mouth and announced at a stage whisper, "Right this minute." *From the joker standing beside me.*

"I'm well aware you're cuttin' the fool at my expense." Bill grunted in derision as he piled Vance's tray with an extra helping of mashed potatoes and gravy. "Fortunately for you, I'm in a charitable mood. Seein' as you're gonna need to keep your strength up to graduate from this place and keep yer day jobs..."

"Burn!" Noah crowed beneath his breath.

"Easy, boys! Easy!" Vance held up his hands in surrender. As he and Noah moved away from the food line with heaping trays, he grumbled, "You were supposed to have my back."

"I'd say we made out pretty well." Noah angled his head at their trays. "Bill might be an old timer, but he's nobody's fool." In some ways, Bill reminded him of his great-uncle. *May he rest in peace.*

"Oh, I see what you're doing." Vance gave a long, low whistle as they took a seat at the nearest vacant table.

"That makes one of us." Noah bowed his head to give a quick, silent prayer of thanks over his food. Then he opened his eyes and dug in.

"Oh, come on." Vance leaned conspiratorially closer after Noah finished praying. "Everyone around us is plotting their survival strategies, and you're no exception. But while they're grabbing the low hanging fruit and forming factions with class-mates, you're playing a longer game — chatting it up with the captain and befriending the cafeteria staff. Gotta hand it to you. That's downright clever."

Noah shook his head, staring at Vance in bemusement. "Sorry to disappoint you, but my only strategy is to work hard and graduate."

"Huh." Vance snorted. "So, I'm supposed to believe it was just an accident you visited with Captain Alicia Downs, one-on-one-oh?"

Noah shrugged. "Would you believe me if I said yes?"

"Don't know," Vance teased. "Still waiting to hear you say it."

Noah cut into his pork chop. "So how'd you know I played football?"

"State championship playoffs," Vance supplied. "Your team lost to mine, remember?"

Nope. Noah remembered losing, but he didn't remember a single player on the opposing team. "Is it just me, or does that feel like a few lifetimes ago?"

"You said it." Vance fist bumped him. "Cop life. It's all glitter and rainbows, isn't it?"

Noah nodded. "What certification are you gunning for here?"

"Urban Rescue. You?"

"Same." Noah wasn't all that surprised. Their

entire class consisted of only fifty students. He was expecting at least eight to ten of them to share his chosen track.

"Wow! Is this the part where we swear a blood oath or something to cooperate and graduate?" Vance's dark gaze twinkled wickedly.

"Not tonight." Noah glanced down at his watch. "Sorry. I have a date."

"You've got to be kidding me! How?" Vance exploded. "You've been here all of what? Two hours?"

"I'm referring to my eighty-two pound Rottweiler," Noah explained dryly.

"Ah." Vance pointed two fingers at his eyes, then aimed them at Noah. "I'll be keeping an eye on you, bro. So, if you're holding out on me about the ladies..."

Smirking, Noah stood with his empty tray. "No way would I do that to a squad mate." He was a get-what-you-see kind of guy. Vance would find that out soon enough.

With another fist bump, they parted ways. After depositing his tray at the clean-up window, Noah took a quick detour to his dorm room to grab a few supplies. He had an idea that he wanted to try out with Java. It was probably a long shot, but it was worth a try.

The dorm room was bustling with talking, laughing classmates. A few seemed to be negotiating bunk bed swaps, probably to get closer to the "factions" Vance had mentioned.

Keeping his head down, Noah retrieved the plastic specimen bag from his storage trunk and stuffed it in the pocket of his jeans. He made his way back to the kennel, mentally forming the last exercise he wanted to put Java through before bedtime. Not only would it potentially help him track down a certain lovely maid — if she was even still on campus this evening — it would also be good practice for the search and rescue training they would begin tomorrow.

Java met him at the door of her cage with a bark of welcome.

"Hey there, Java-kins." He unlocked the cage and let himself inside, glad to see her food bowl was empty. He was even more glad not to detect any messes on the floor. She'd kept her meal down this time, meaning he'd chosen a dog food brand that she liked. *One hurdle crossed.* There would be many more in the coming days, but this one was a biggie.

Java pranced around him, nosing at his pockets in search of treats.

"Patience, girl." He removed the specimen bag from his pocket and carefully pulled apart the zipper seal. Crouching down, he held it open so she could sniff at the pink cleaning cloth. With any luck, it would still have some of Farrah Carmichael's scent clinging to it.

To his amazement, the dog immediately pressed her nose to the ground and started to snuffle in a jagged motion. From the way she was acting, he could only presume she'd picked up on Farrah's scent.

"Really?" Noah demanded. "You sure about that?" Curious as to where Java's nose would lead her, he attached her leash and opened the door of her cage.

She sniffed her way down the hallway toward the administrative offices in the back.

"Not what I had in mind, but okay." He followed her, fairly certain that she'd lost the target scent — or had never picked it up in the first place. Maybe it was too masked by the disinfectant spray fumes.

However, Java seemed so intent on her search that Noah hated to interrupt her. Whatever she was smelling, disinfectant spray or otherwise, she was following it.

The door to the first administrative office abruptly opened, and he found himself staring at the same woman who'd occupied way too many of his thoughts throughout the evening. She looked as astonished as he felt.

Java pranced forward, yipping triumphantly at Farrah Carmichael's heels.

"Nice going, Java!" Noah rewarded her with a milk bone. "Sit. Stay." He straightened to face the owner of the cleaning cloth.

"Hey, Bloom."

Her lips parted, and a whole range of expressions flooded her heart-shaped features — disbelief, irritation, and some other emotion he was at a loss to describe. Two pink spots rose to her cheeks.

"Did you seriously make me the target of your latest dog training shenanigans?"

He shrugged sheepishly. "Whatever the right answer to your question is, that's what I'm going with."

"You're unbelievable." She leaned closer to snatch the pink cloth out of his hand and proceeded to use it to wipe down the doorknob of the office.

He glanced curiously around her, wondering where the rest of her cleaning supplies were. The office lights were turned off behind her, making it difficult to make out much of anything in the darkness. "I take it you work evenings here?"

"Sure do." Unless he was mistaken, her voice held a tinge of nervousness.

He wished he could think of something to say to alleviate the awkwardness settling between them. "So, ah...thanks for being such a good sport about our tracking exercise. Being a new dog owner and all, I wasn't sure if it would even work."

She shook her head at him. "You are completely shameless, Noah Zeller."

"I know." He held her gaze, every bit as enchanted by the flustered version of her as he had been by the smart-mouthed version of her earlier. "If I wasn't about to start a month of hell in the morning, I'd press my luck further and ask you out. Right now."

"Noah," she squeaked, blushing. "We can't. That is..."

"Right." His heart sank at her response. It wasn't the least bit encouraging. "No fraternizing with the staff. I seem to remember reading that somewhere." He was surprised the policy extended to the cleaning staff, though. Was it just her way of letting him down easily?

"Yeah. Something like that." She glanced away, still blushing.

He swallowed his disappointment, but it wasn't easy. "Maybe some other time, Farrah." He dropped her real name on purpose, wanting to see her reaction.

She jolted. "How did you know my—?"

"I ran into your mom at the pet store."

"Ah!" Her slender shoulders stiffened. "I should've known she wouldn't stay at home and rest like she was supposed to. Did she seem alright?"

"Yep."

Farrah's eyelashes fluttered against her cheeks. "Did she say anything about me?"

"Like what?" He was enjoying teasing her way too much.

"Anything," she snapped.

"Yeah. She's sorry you're having to cover for her while she's injured." He leaned closer, drawling, "Is there anything in particular your evening shift is keeping you from? Or anyone?"

A breathy chuckle escaped her. "Wouldn't you like to know?"

"Actually, yeah." Sometimes going for the truth was the best way to keep another person off balance. "Very much."

CHAPTER 4: NO MERCY

FARRAH

Farrah set her alarm for bright and early the next morning. She'd had a little trouble sleeping last night, which she blamed entirely on Police Detective Noah Zeller.

Holy cow! She still couldn't believe he'd asked her out. *Or made it clear he wants to.* Pressing a hand to her racing heart, she recalled his intense brown gaze that always made her feel like he saw more than she wanted him to.

She was accustomed to being flirted with, but never before had any man included his canine partner in the efforts. It was both a diabolically clever and heart-stoppingly sweet gesture. *Gosh!* If he was genuinely trying to get her attention, he sure had succeeded.

He was also fast proving her first impression of him wrong. She'd been so sure he was a newbie on the brink of crashing and burning, one of those hotheads who thought they knew everything until the hard core SAR instructors set them straight. After last night's stunt, however, she was starting to think he might have what it took to brave the rigors of search and rescue training. Even more disturbing was the fact that she was inwardly rooting for him to do exactly that.

It was an emotion she would have to hide during today's training, no matter how difficult a task it proved to be.

Lord, give me strength. She donned the staff uniform she'd been issued, trying not to think about the fact that Noah's broody eyes would be focused one hundred percent on her this morning — at least during the parts of the training she would be facilitating.

She was sort of dying to see his reaction when he realized she was Captain Alicia Downs' intern. *I am capable of so much more than cleaning up your doggy messes, detective.* She was standing where she was today — in a private instructor's cabin — because she'd earned the right to be here. She'd earned it through high grades, two college degrees, and hard work every step of the way. Her dog grooming days were well behind her. She was upping her game to the next level, baby!

Every few minutes, she had to pinch herself to make sure she wasn't dreaming. Her hands trembled slightly as she finger-combed her hair into a ponytail and mashed her black ball cap on. *I can do this!* She wasn't just doing it for herself. She was also doing it for her mother, who'd made countless sacrifices to put her through college. Someday, she was going to repay those sacrifices, maybe by purchasing her a new car or something.

Too uptight to eat breakfast, Farrah paid a visit to the coffee bar in the lobby of the main auditorium. It held a trio of coffee makers, the kind that dispensed one cup at a time. Shoving an empty cup beneath the first dispenser, she mashed a few buttons to select the desired size and flavor. Lifting the freshly brewed hazelnut coffee to her lips, she took small sips, allowing it to work its magic on her overwrought nerves.

She strolled to the glassed-in showcase just outside the double doors of the auditorium, eyeing the framed photographs of the current staff members. The training center's commander's stern expression and unyielding profile brought to mind a general. He'd made hundreds of other students tremble in their boots, and was about to make a few dozen more do so today. He understood that the skills they taught at the center would all too often be employed in life or death situations after graduation.

That's why he worked so hard to make the training feel like it was real. The campus housed state-of-the-art simulations of nearly every major calamity caused by fire, natural disasters, and humans. There were additional specialized courses available in tracking and scenting, narcotics discovery and recovery, cadaver searches, bomb detection, the search and rescue of missing persons, as well as patrol and sentry best practices.

"When were you going to tell me about your extra evening duties with the cleaning staff?" Captain Alicia Downs' voice grated in Farrah's ears.

She glanced over at the instructor's scowling expression. *Never, I guess.* "Don't worry, ma'am. I've worked two or more jobs for as long as I can remember. It won't affect my performance as an intern."

"Of course it will," her new boss snarled. "From where I stand, that kind of hard work is what got you here."

Though Farrah appreciated her kind words, she hastened to assure the woman. "If for any reason you require my assistance during my cleaning shift, I'll find someone to cover for me." *Either that, or I'll lose even more sleep catching up in the middle of the night.* She'd promised her mother she'd cover that two hour span, and she intended to keep her word.

"Of course I'm not going to require your assistance during those hours," the captain blustered. "But I might have if I didn't know about your situation. Now that we're working together, I need to know about stuff like that."

"Understood, ma'am."

Her boss nodded. "Let's head to the stage entrance. It's about time for us to make our first appearance."

They crossed the foyer and headed down a long hallway to reach the side entrance to the stage. On their way, they passed several clusters of students.

Out of the corner of her eye, Farrah caught sight of Noah standing next to a fellow student the size of a lumberjack. Wow! It was as if the guy had been built to strike fear into the hearts of criminals.

She kept her face averted as she and the captain passed by them. To her dismay, Alicia Downs paused to address Noah.

"Did you sleep in the kennel like I suggested, detective?"

Though Farrah kept walking, she heard Noah's rumbly baritone response. "I'm ready for your training, ma'am." It was a respectful sidestep of the question that Farrah knew the answer to. He had not slept in the dog kennel. She couldn't fathom why her boss had even suggested it.

"We'll see about that." Alicia Downs' response was clipped. She caught up with Farrah. "You seem in an awful hurry to get out there on stage."

"What can I say, ma'am?" Farrah returned in a light voice. "I'm looking forward to getting started on our first training session."

She and her boss joined the rest of the instructors backstage. According to a large white poster clipped to an easel, they would be marching out to the stage in two even rows.

The captain sniffed. "You can tell the training center is being run by former soldiers." She sounded more amused than critical.

Farrah couldn't disagree. She also couldn't help wondering if the training center was eyeing the captain for a more permanent position in their ranks.

An instructor Farrah didn't recognize signaled that it was time for them to make their appearance in front of the students gathered in the auditorium. Silence fell over their group as they filed on stage.

At first, the spotlights were too blinding for Farrah to see much. However, her eyesight soon adjusted enough for her to make out a sea of faces. When the training center's commander started to speak, all other lights on stage dimmed. He remained alone in the spotlight.

At this point, Farrah was able to see the students much more clearly — enough to determine that Noah Zeller was sitting in the front row. He was staring right at her with an inscrutable expression.

She stared back, feeling more than a little dazed by the amazing opportunity she was embarking on today. Okay, maybe a little of that dazed feeling was coming from the intensity of Noah's gaze. She wished she knew what he was thinking. Was he surprised to discover she was more than an hourly worker on the cleaning staff?

Glad? Disappointed? Indifferent? It was impossible for her to tell.

The giddy thought crossed her mind that he'd asked her out before he knew the truth about her employment status. *Points for you, Noah Zeller. Big points!* It was nice to know he was attracted to who she was more than what she did for a living.

The rest of the opening ceremony passed in a blur beneath his unwavering brown gaze. His square jaw was set, his lips clamped in a determined line. Farrah idly wondered what it would be like to feel that hard mouth on hers. Then she gave herself a mental kick for entertaining such a crazy thought. Noah was about to become one of her students, for pity's sake. She wasn't supposed to be imagining stuff like that about him.

Since he'd wanted to ask her out last night, though, she had to assume he was wondering the same thing about her. Heat rose to her cheeks. *Oh, my lands! Just stop!*

Since it was decent weather, Captain Alicia Downs was holding their first training session outside. She'd briefed Farrah in great detail about today's curriculum during yesterday's planning meeting. They'd even toured the training course together. Farrah had been tickled to death to discover that the captain hadn't brought her on board to serve as a glorified errand girl. She expected Farrah to be an extension of her own eyes and ears while the trainees and their dogs worked their way through each urban disaster simulation.

Their squad consisted of only four students, and not for lack of sign-ups. Apparently, Captain Alicia Downs had a waiting list a mile long for her training courses. However, the training center's officials — for reasons they weren't advertising — had only selected four highly qualified candidates. These three men and one woman had been pulled from the regular Urban Rescue course to participate in her elite, military-grade version of the training. It would culminate in a five-day, full immersion experience in an urban warfare setting. Farrah could only assume the center was experimenting with a new curriculum that they weren't ready to fully roll out yet.

To alleviate the disappointment of the candidates who weren't selected for the captain's special squad, the center had her scheduled for a series of surprise visits to the other programs of study throughout the coming weeks. During these sessions, Farrah would be expected to solely cover the special clinic. *Wowsers!* It made no sense to her that they'd brought in a new college graduate for such an enormous responsibility, as opposed to hiring a more experienced professional. However, she wasn't complaining about their decision.

Returning her attention to their small huddle, Farrah was awash with gratitude all over again at being chosen to be part of such an elite team. Police

Detective Noah Zeller certainly looked the part this morning. His uniform was freshly pressed, his features unsmiling. She wished she could read his expression, but it was impossible to see his eyes beneath the visor of his uniform cap and the same pair of aviator sunglasses he'd worn during their first encounter. The single, most remarkable thing about his appearance, however, wasn't his poker face and immaculate appearance. It was his canine partner.

His barking, prancing dog of yesterday had been transformed into an obedient sentry at his side. The change in Java was so dramatic that it was uncanny. The Rottweiler observed the people and other dogs around her with a patient, unblinking stare. Farrah could almost see the wheels spinning inside her furry head as she assessed her surroundings and registered no immediate threat.

"Alright, trainees. This is the moment you've been waiting for." Captain Alicia Downs stepped forward to address her squad. "Welcome to day one of the Texas Hotline Training Center's Urban Rescue Training Program. If you expected to start off with flying bullets and screaming sirens, you won't be disappointed." She tapped a finger against the face of her watch. "That part is coming right after we introduce ourselves."

A brief round of chuckles met her words. They quickly faded when there was no answering smile from her. She hadn't shown up to amuse them or be amused. Her students snapped to full alert mode.

The captain fixed her gaze on Noah first. "Police Detective Noah Zeller and I have already met. His partner is Java. They have a combined twelve years of search and rescue experience in the Houston area. Not together, mind you. They are new partners, which should be interesting. Do you have anything to add to that, Trainee Zeller?"

He shook his head. "That covers it, ma'am."

She nodded at him and Java, giving them one last hard look before moving on to the man standing beside him. "Police Sergeant Vance Briggs is from Dallas. Though we haven't yet met, I'm told his biggest accomplishment was winning the state play-offs with his high school football team, incidentally defeating Police Detective Noah Zeller's team. Since this happened a full decade ago, we'll see how far that trophy gets him in this course."

Vance's dark features first registered amazement, then grudging respect. Farrah could tell that the captain's unorthodox introduction had caught him off guard. He quickly recovered his normal level of cockiness, nudging Noah in the ribs with his elbow as if the two of them shared a private joke.

"His canine partner bears the somewhat unoriginal name of Bomber," the captain continued, "but we'll let that pass." She paused dramatically, then added, "For now."

Farrah watched as Vance's wide mouth dissolved into an *ooh* of mock dismay. It looked to her like he was enjoying his instructor's harsh criticism. His all-white Doberman Pinscher, who resembled a ghost more than a dog, chose that exact moment to let his long pink tongue loll out of his mouth. It was such a comical sight that it was all Farrah could do not to laugh out loud.

"I'm not going to ask if Trainee Briggs has anything to add to his story, because we don't have all day." Amidst another round of chuckles, the captain moved on to their only female trainee, a willowy blonde with her hair pulled back in a tight bun. Her face was heavily freckled from over-exposure to the sun. She could have been twenty-five, thirty-five, or forty-five. It was impossible to tell behind her tinted sunglasses.

"Penny Jump is not a law enforcement officer like our first two students. For those of you who are wondering...no, that isn't her real name. Yes, she'd have to kill you if she told you the truth about her identity."

Though the comment was met by a few smirks, Farrah honestly couldn't tell whether or not her new boss was joking.

"She specializes in skydiving from perfectly good airplanes," Alicia Downs continued in the same matter-of-fact tone. "She also rappels from perfectly good choppers. As you can imagine, she has descended into a number of highly tense situations. Those she rescued will forever be grateful to her. This month, she'll be training with a canine partner named Dive. I believe there's a pun intended somewhere in that."

Farrah watched Penny's sun-kissed hand drop to rest on the head of her German Shepherd. The dog instinctively leaned closer to her handler. Farrah could only imagine the level of rapport it had taken to train the dog to go on tandem jumps. She'd not seen the two of them in action yet, but she couldn't wait to.

Captain Downs waved to their final squad member, a short sturdy fellow with a shock of thick, dark hair waving out from beneath his cap. "This is Doc, a medic who was embedded with the 75th Army Ranger Battalion for the past six years. He has a real name, but no one ever uses it. Like Penny, he'd have to axe you if he talked about his experience, so we'll just let your imaginations fill in the blanks. I don't mind sharing that he's the proud owner of not one, but two purple hearts for wounds sustained in battle. His faithful canine partner, Juice, has served with him for the past two years. I imagine there's a story behind his dog's name that I, for one, look forward to hearing."

Farrah couldn't wait to hear it, as well. Juice was a Golden Retriever with a friendly face befitting a canine angel of mercy.

The captain started to walk away. Then she abruptly pivoted to face Doc and Juice again. "Though we are grateful for your service to our nation, let me be painfully clear about this. Your past accomplishments will have no bearing on your grade in this course. That goes for all of you." The air seemed to settle more heavily on the group as she paced in front of them, giving each of them a hard once-over. "The harsh reality is that the world of search and rescue operations is only interested in what you and your canine partner can do today to help the innocent victims out there." She pointed vaguely toward the parking lot, but Farrah knew she was referring to the hometowns where the students served and would soon be returning to.

Next, the captain glanced over at Farrah with a barely perceptible nod.

Farrah slid her thumb over the start button on the remote control in her hand and moved to stand behind a tall set of silver portable stairs. They were mounted on tiny wheels.

"In our first exercise," the captain pointed at the enormous pile of rubble in the field behind them, "a group of homeland terrorists has claimed responsibility for detonating this building. Our bomb squad has identified and dismantled the remaining two bombs. Or so we've been told. Let's hope and pray their report is accurate. As the first response team, your job is to search the rubble for two VIP hostages.

Their scent specimens are located in the two silver canisters at the base of the stairs that Intern Carmichael is rolling into position."

Farrah mashed the button on her remote control, and the hidden emergency sirens started to scream. She watched all four students and their dogs jolt. This was the first test — to see how they would react to the unexpected. Real emergencies rarely came with a preliminary warning. They simply rained down their horror without mercy.

Captain Alicia Downs flipped on her lapel microphone and started to bellow, "Let's move! Let's move! Let's move!"

Farrah finished pushing the silver stairs across the bumpy stretch of grass.

Noah and Vance sprinted her way and added their strength to hers. Whether by design or by accident, Noah's callused fingers brushed hers during the exchange. She stepped back the moment the stairs were in position. For the rest of the exercise, her role would be a hands-off one. She would strictly observe the performance of the others.

A quick glance to her left proved that the other two trainees already had their dogs' muzzles inside the scent specimen canisters.

Noah and Vance continued to hold the stairs steady while Penny and Doc mounted them first. Penny's German Shepherd bounded up the open-sided stairs without hesitation, but Doc's Golden

Retriever took them a little more slowly. As he neared the top, he paused and glanced over the side at the long drop below him. Doc regained his attention with a sharp whistle and drove him onward.

Captain Downs joined Farrah at the base of the stairs when Noah and Vance finished scaling them with their dogs. "Come on!" she urged, waving at Farrah to follow her.

They jogged up the stairs after the trainees. At the top, Captain Downs motioned for them to fan out across the rubble. Then she marched determinedly after Penny and Doc. Taking the cue, Farrah directed her attention to Noah and Vance.

As she picked her way painstakingly across the wide, jagged slabs of concrete and twisted metal, a hissing sound warned her that she'd tripped one of the hidden chlorine bombs. Roughly the consistency of swimming pool water, they were essentially harmless. The color of her dyed hair, however, was in extreme jeopardy.

"Get down!" she shrieked to the two men, leaping away from the blast to huddle against the ground with her hands over her head.

Though their black uniforms were spattered with droplets that would soon fade the fabric to a lighter color, Farrah was relieved to find her hair remained dry. Whipping off her ball cap, she ran her hands over the sides of her head and down the length of her ponytail to be sure.

Noah Zeller lunged in her direction. "Are you alright?" He reached for her, looking alarmed. His hands lightly closed around her wrists. "Where does it hurt?"

Java followed him, barking excitedly at Farrah's ankles.

"I'm fine. Just a little wigged out over the not-so-amazing effects chlorine can have on hair dye." She gently shook off his hands, her heart racing over the way his six feet of holy hunkiness was towering protectively over her.

Concern was etched across the hard planes and angles of his face for a moment longer. Then he broke into a chuckle, glancing away. "Really, Farrah?"

"Really, Trainee Zeller." It was her job to remind him of their roles.

His head suddenly snapped back in her direction. "If you don't mind me asking, what color did your hair start off as?"

"I mind." She motioned with both hands for him to return to the exercise. "I think our hostage situation takes precedence over everything else right now, including my choice of hair colors." She and her mother had been dying their hair a shade of honey-brown for as long as she could remember. No doubt it was one of the reasons they were forever being mistaken for sisters, something that both of them got an enormous kick out of.

"Fine. We can circle back to it later."

When he didn't immediately return to the training exercise, she hissed, "What's it to you, anyway?"

"I already gave you my reasons, Intern Carmichael." With a final searching look at her, he whistled for Java to follow him as they carefully worked their way across the rubble to Vance's side.

She stared after him in wonder. Yesterday, she'd assumed he was at least half-joking about asking her out. However, he sure didn't sound like it today.

No, Police Detective Noah Zeller had just finished making his feelings on the topic perfectly clear. Apparently, he didn't give a rip if she was a maid, an intern, or a recent arrival from Mars.

He wants to date me. For real!

CHAPTER 5: THE PLOT THICKENS

NOAH

"Over here!" Vance shouted, waving both hands wildly at Noah.

Noah picked up his pace as he retraced his steps across the broken slabs of concrete. He crouched beside his classmate to help him remove a pile of rubble from the man pinned below it. They swiftly uncovered a dummy wearing a dusty black business suit. They'd found the first VIP. Apparently, the terrorists had decided they no longer needed their hostages.

Since the place where they were crouched was stable, Noah and Vance didn't move the body for fear of worsening any potential head or neck injuries. Instead, Noah called in the medical evacuation crew.

A helicopter rumbled in the distance. He shaded his eyes, wondering if it was merely a coincidence.

Nope. The chopper was definitely cruising their way.

Vance leaned closer to him as the aircraft approached. "Nice of you to part with your woman long enough to come lend me a hand over here."

"No idea what you're talking about," Noah drawled.

"Liar." Vance sobered, running a hand over his sweaty forehead. "Is she okay?"

"Yep. Just worried about her hair dye, apparently."

Vance snorted as he unbuttoned his cuffs and rolled up his sleeves. "I see the two of you are keeping your convos strictly professional. Nothing to worry about there."

Noah's gaze landed on the tiny set of footprints tattooed to the inside of Vance's forearm. "What's it to you, Daddy-O? Looks like your heart is already spoken for."

"Three times over." Vance shoved his sleeve a few inches higher, so he could get a better look.

Noah stared in amazement at the three sets of footprints. A name was scrawled beneath each one — Adele, Brooke, and Cecily. "You're the father of triplets?" With the way Vance had been acting, Noah had pegged him for a single guy.

Vance shrugged and lowered his arm. "I believe in getting stuff done, bro. Boom! Instant family. No messing around."

"How old are they?" Noah couldn't have been more fascinated.

"Two. Best two-and-a-half years of my life." Vance craned his neck to watch the helicopter rumble closer.

Once it was hovering above their heads, a pair of medical workers slid down a pair of ropes with a stretcher clutched between them. They shouted the usual questions to Noah and Vance about the condition of the victim. The medical team then went through the motions of taking the dummy's vitals. Afterward, they strapped him to their stretcher and signaled for their comrades to lift him into the chopper.

By the time the lunch hour rolled around, Captain Alicia Downs and her students were filthy, their clothing was permanently torn and stained, and they were physically beat. However, she had them continue to stand vigil until the final hostage was hauled away in an ambulance.

Then she called for them to huddle up at the base of the rubble. "We'll do our debriefing after lunch. You're going to need to hustle to the cafeteria. They're only going to be open for about another twenty minutes."

As Noah and his classmates exchanged weary glances, she added briskly, "We'll reconvene in classroom two oh six. Come prepared to take notes. Oh, and keep your dogs kenneled for the next session. They've earned a little siesta."

She motioned for Farrah to remain with her. Noah watched them retreat in the direction of the staff cabins. Lucky them! It looked like they were going to get showers.

With another wry glance at each other, he and his classmates broke into a jog as they made a beeline for the kennel. Fortunately, there were two staff members on duty who promised to feed, water, and cage the dogs for them.

There were a mere ten minutes of their lunch hour remaining when Noah, Vance, Penny, and Doc finally made it to the food line.

Bill was stationed behind the glass again. He eyed their bedraggled state without any change in his expression.

Vance jutted his chin at him. "Sounds like you and the captain shot the breeze about football last night."

"Did I?" Bill's grizzled features adopted a smug expression. "I talk to a lot of people. No way I can remember every conversation." He busied himself filling their trays with mountainous servings of nachos, rice, and beans.

"State playoffs," Vance pressed. "My team versus this bad boy's team from Houston." He lightly bumped shoulders with Noah.

"Nah," Bill drawled lazily. "Not ringin' a bell."

Noah shook his head at Vance's loud whoop over the heaping tray of nachos Bill handed him. "Any chance I can get mine to go, sir?"

"As a matter of fact." With a flourish, the older gentleman withdrew a white to-go box from beneath the counter and loaded it to the gills with nachos.

Noah gave a huff of appreciation. "Do you accept tips?"

"Not from cops." Bill's voice was edged with iron. "No, sireee! Can't tell you how much I appreciate you young-uns keeping the streets safe for us older folks."

"Oh, hey!" Vance crowed, eying the to-go box with delight. "Got any more of those boxes? Sure wouldn't mind taking one to class."

Glancing in the opposite direction, Bill stuck a finger in his ear and wiggled it. "Dumb old ears. They sure get to rattling sometimes."

Noah gave Vance a shove between the shoulder blades to keep the line moving. "I feel your pain, sir. My ears have been rattling ever since a certain police sergeant crossed my path yesterday."

Vance's upper lip curled. "I make your life richer."

Noah leaned closer to Vance's ear. "You keep telling yourself that, sergeant."

"I'm not the one who needs convincing," his classmate shot back.

"Eh, quit your sulking." They headed for one of

the empty lunch tables, but Noah decided to keep moving. "Actually, I need to squeeze in an errand. Don't cry too hard for me while I'm gone."

Vance's gaze flickered to the to-go box Noah was holding. "When are you gonna eat?"

"In class, I hope." Noah nodded at several class-mates from other programs whose mouths were gaping at his squad's sorely bedraggled appearance.

"As long as Captain Ironsides Downs allows it," Vance growled. "You sure you want to take that chance?"

"I'm sure." Noah had been mulling over his missing persons case all morning. He needed to retrieve his case files to take a closer look at the artist renditions of the estranged daughter of Bram Carstens. She wouldn't have changed near as dramatically as her daughter during the past twenty-five years.

"Alright," Vance sighed, "but don't say I didn't warn you when you're face planting into the tulips this afternoon from sheer lack of fuel."

"I'll find someone else to blame," Noah promised with a smirk.

He hurried back to their dorm room, all too aware of the ever ticking clock. A guy from one of the other programs was actually napping. *Must be nice, Sleeping Beauty.* Noah resisted the urge to kick the legs of his bed on his way past it.

Unlocking his storage trunk, he reached for his

case files. He was too filthy to sit on the bed, so he opted to perch atop the closed lid of his trunk. Setting the box of nachos beside him, he quickly thumbed through the first folder.

And there was the picture he was looking for.

Bram Carstens' only daughter stared back at him from her yellowed photograph. Nadine Carstens had been pregnant with her daughter, Farrah, at the time. Her belly was swollen, her strawberry blonde hair tousled, and her expression angry from the disagreement she'd supposedly had with her father over her lack of interest in the family business. They'd also argued over the fact that she'd refused to divulge the name of her unborn child's father.

Only hours after her baby was born, she'd checked herself out of the hospital against her doctor's orders and disappeared, taking her infant daughter with her. Two short years later, her death certificate had surfaced. She'd perished in a freak car explosion. There'd been very little to scrape up afterward.

Every inquiry of Bram Carstens into the matter had resulted in the same answer. No one knew much about the late woman's two-year-old daughter, though several people testified that she'd been toying with the idea of adopting her out.

But what if she hadn't followed through? Noah's gaze narrowed on the old photograph. What if he and everyone else had been looking at this case all wrong? What if they'd been following a trail of purposefully placed bread crumbs, specifically designed to lead them away from the truth?

If he erased all of his previous assumptions, he was left with a few very interesting theories — including one in which Nadine Carstens had not, in fact, died in the mysterious fire. She'd wanted to be left alone to chart her own course. And what better way to do that than to fake her own death and start over?

Convincing the authorities to declare her dead would've been a tricky matter, but not impossible. It would have taken something like teeth, a metal implant, or some other form of irrefutable identification.

Noah riffled through the papers in his file, searching for anything that would fit that description. When he found it, he had to shake his head. It was so obvious that it was laughable. Nadine's body had been identified by a single tooth. A wisdom tooth, to be more precise. Though it was charred, enough DNA had been extracted from it to produce a clear forensic fingerprint.

According to the testimony of her parents, her wisdom teeth had never fully formed, so they'd never been extracted. Unless Nadine herself had paid to remove them for the sole purpose of planting one at the scene of the fire.

Feeling like he was on to something solid, Noah

shot a text message off to Police Chief Hector Manning. *We need to run more artist renditions of the present-day Nadine Carstens.*

Since Noah didn't have time to explain further, he could only hope that the police chief would read between the lines for the rest of his message. He was approaching the case from a new angle — one which presumed Nadine had lived.

Noah locked the case files back in his trunk. It was funny how he might never have questioned the death of Bram Carstens' daughter if it weren't for his somewhat pointless conversation with Farrah about hair color.

It had gotten him thinking. If Nadine was still alive, she would've probably done a number of things — acquired a fake ID, left town, and adopted a new appearance. Dying her hair would have been one of the easiest ways to accomplish that.

NOAH WOULD'VE LIKED to spend more time combing through the case files, but the last few minutes of his lunch break flew by too quickly. He had to sprint to make it to class on time. He slid into the chair closest to the door just as Captain Downs was standing to start their next session.

"Cutting it a little close, are we, Trainee Zeller?" She paced across the front of the classroom like a general surveying her troops. Farrah was perched at a teacher's desk by the windows. Three semi-circles of tables completed the classroom.

Noah and his classmates were all seated in the front row. He nodded at their instructor to acknowledge her words. However, he saw no reason to grovel or apologize for being on time.

She gave the air a tentative sniff as her gaze zoomed in on the white boxes sitting in front of each student. "Well, that's one way to mask your stench, trainees."

Noah appreciated their show of solidarity. By everyone marching to class with a to-go box, it wasn't as obvious that he was the only one who hadn't yet eaten.

Vance caught his eye and shot him a thumbs up.

Noah pressed a fist to his chest, knowing his brother in blue must have engineered the clever little feat.

"Then again," Captain Downs mused, watching the by-play between the cops, "this could be construed as a subtle complaint about how short your lunch break was. Trainee Briggs." She rounded on him, "would you like to file a complaint?"

"No, ma'am!" His expression was a portrait of respect. He gingerly touched the skin beneath his eyes. "I assure you, these are tears of joy." His face was dry. "Or sweat. I'm not a hundred percent sure which."

"Laying it on a little thick there, Briggs." Her voice was dry as she waved at his box of nachos. "The sooner you get back to eating, the sooner the rest of us can quit listening to your nonsense."

Taking that as her permission to chow down, he happily opened the lid of his box and dug in to his second round of nachos. Noah had long since come to the conclusion that the guy was a bottomless pit.

After a few bites, Penny slid her box in Vance's direction. He accepted it with a happy grin.

Noah scarfed down the contents of his own box. Man, but he was famished! He and his classmates had worked up real appetites this morning.

Captain Downs motioned for Farrah to take the floor next. She backed up to the desk Farrah vacated to hike one hip on the edge of it. Folding her arms, she watched her intern with interest.

Farrah addressed the class. "As Captain Downs mentioned this morning, I'm Intern Farrah Carmichael, an Animal Behaviorist with a Masters Degree in Animal Behavior. I'm also a certified service dog trainer and certified dog handler. Welcome to our first after-action review." As she strolled across the front of the room, two things were immediately apparent.

Neither she nor the captain had taken the time to shower or change, as he originally presumed they would. They were as filthy as him and his classmates. Secondly, she carried herself with supreme confidence. She knew dogs inside and out. It was no surprise she'd been selected for such a prestigious internship. Noah wondered what her career aspirations were. He doubted they included serving as a maid much longer.

"Captain Downs will coach and critique your skills as a search and rescue expert. I will be observing and offering advice on the performance of your dogs." She paused her pacing to stand in front of Penny Jump.

"Trainee Jump, how about you start us off by naming two strengths and two weakness, if any, that you observed in Dive today."

Penny frowned in concentration. "Dive isn't easily rattled by noise and commotion. Like everyone else around her, she jolted when the sirens went off, but she's trained for situations like that. She immediately went into SAR mode. She didn't hesitate to climb the portable stairs. Heights are kind of our specialty." She smiled faintly. "However, sometimes I worry that she's been over-trained."

Farrah looked intrigued by her last statement. "Can you expound on that, Trainee Jump?"

"Absolutely. She's been desensitized to so many things that she just charges straight into the jaws of danger. I'm afraid that tendency could really end up costing us."

"How?" Farrah pressed.

Penny waved a hand. "The chlorine bombs, for

instance. It was only a training exercise today, but we'll be returning to the real world soon where far worse things will detonate. I've put her through a number of programs designed to re-sensitize her, but none of them have had any effect."

"They're not going to," Farrah informed her. "I'm not convinced that's the answer you're looking for, at any rate."

"You're right, ma'am." Penny ran a hand over her windblown hair to smooth back the loose strands. "Her fearlessness is what makes it possible for her to leap out of aircrafts with me."

"Which leaves you with only one other solution, right?"

Penny looked surprised. "You mean me."

"Bingo." Farrah's smile was so warm with compassion that Noah could have hugged her. "You're the dog handler. You make the calls. With that in mind, how should you solve this dilemma?"

Noah was impressed by how Farrah wasn't in a hurry to just hand over the answers. She was guiding Penny towards figuring things out for herself.

"Well..." Penny pondered the question for a moment. "My search and rescue dog's performance is the product of both our rapport and her response to my commands."

"Which you continuously rehearse," Farrah noted.

"Yes." Penny's expression brightened. "So, I need

to come up with a new command. One that entails tracking and heeling at the same time. A more controlled version of tracking, if you will."

"Exactly!" Farrah waved a finger triumphantly. "I recommend you start working with Dive on it today. You and she have an entire month to practice this new skill under the tutelage of the country's finest dog handlers. If it were me, I'd take advantage of that resource."

"Thank you. I can't wait to get started."

Farrah moved to stand in front of Vance next. "Talk to us about Bomber, Trainee Briggs. What are his strengths and weaknesses?" Her lips quirked upward. "There are extra points riding on any answers you give that don't contain football references."

"Easy now, Intern Carmichael." His dark gaze twinkled at her. "The toughest thing about Bomber is living up to his name. He has no idea he's a Doberman Pinscher. If anything, he thinks he's a teddy bear."

His words were met with chuckles. "Fortunately, his loyalty to me supersedes his fears. It is my belief that he would face a firing squad in an attempt to save me."

She nodded. "That's the definition of true bravery, in my book — the ability to rise above one's own fears to get the job done."

"True." Vance didn't look entirely convinced.

"But, like Doc's dog, his timidness about heights slowed us down today on the stairs. In a real emergency, every second counts."

"So, what are you going to do about it?"

"Train through it," he supplied. "It's the only way for him to move forward from here."

"How?"

"Maybe get him out on more obstacle courses to help him overcome his fears."

She fluttered a hand at their classroom windows, which overlooked the east training fields. "In case you are not aware, over ninety percent of the training center's facilities are open to you and your dogs after hours. Feel free to use them for additional training. The only exception are the virtual simulation labs."

"Roger that." Vance nodded.

"What about when you return to the police department?" she prodded.

"Our training needs to continue," he said simply.

"It never ends," she agreed. Next, she addressed a scenting and tracking issue with Doc. Apparently, Juice was easily sidetracked. They discussed various methods for keeping her on task.

She saved Noah for last. "I hope your beautiful Rottweiler didn't suffer any chlorine stains to her coat this morning, detective."

"She's A-okay, ma'am." He wasn't sure what she was getting at.

"Good." She reached out to lightly knock on the

table in front of him as she passed by. "Chlorine can be death on certain shades of brown as well as strawberry blonde." She paused a moment to let that sink in.

Strawberry blonde? Was that her way of disclosing her real hair color to him? Noah studied her lovely features, imagining them framed in strawberry blonde hair. The picture that formed in his mind looked surprisingly like Nadine Carstens from twenty-five years ago — minus the puffiness from her pregnancy.

"You know the drill, detective," Farrah continued smoothly. "Let's chat about Java's strengths and weaknesses."

He was momentarily tongue-tied as the dots inside his head connected to form yet another theory. What if the missing woman he'd been searching for was standing directly in front of him?

CHAPTER 6: DANCE OF HEARTS

NOAH

At the conclusion of their first day of training, Farrah handed out a short survey to Noah and his class mates. The last question had an area to write in comments and suggestions. He left a comment praising the setup of the kennels. Carefully under-lining the word *kennel*, he jabbed his finger at the word as he turned in his survey to her.

She hastily scanned his answers. "Excellent, Trainee Zeller. I highly recommend you invest your time in another training session with Java after dinner."

His heart pounded at the knowledge that she'd not only understood his request, she was additionally agreeing to meet with him. *It's a date, beautiful.* She'd even given him a time.

The moment Captain Downs dismissed them, he headed straight for the dorm to grab a shower. No way was he showing up to see Farrah with a day's worth of muck and grime caked beneath his finger-nails. He hoped she liked cowboys, because jeans and boots were all he'd packed. It was a sunny evening, so he kept his shades on until he reached the cafeteria.

Penny sashayed neatly into the food line ahead of him. Her long blonde hair was down this evening. She tossed a handful of it over her shoulder as she stepped closer to him. "It's nice to be clean again, isn't it?"

"Yup." He eyed her warily, sensing she wanted something from him.

She glanced furtively over her shoulder. "I have a favor to ask."

Here it comes.

She wrinkled her nose at him. "As luck would have it, my ex is here in the room."

He raised his eyebrows at her. "A fellow class-mate or a staff member?"

"Classmate," she supplied coolly. "One who has expressed an interest in getting back together."

"I'm happy for you," he returned blandly, wondering what any of this had to do with him.

"He's expressed his interest annoyingly and repeatedly." Her gaze narrowed with resentment. "That's where you come in. I was kind of hoping you and I could pretend to be—"

"Can't." He spared her a tight smile. "I'm going

to have to sit this one out." Any canoodling with Penny, fake or real, could blow his chances with Farrah. He couldn't afford that, not even to help out a classmate.

"I thought you were single." She pouted.

"It's complicated." Apparently, her life was complicated, too. He didn't mind extending a little sympathy, but he was in no position to pick up her troubles and carry them.

"I knew it!" Vance leaned around Noah to jab a large finger at him. "You've been holding out on us, man. What's her name?" He was all showered up and sharp looking in an untucked navy polo, jeans, and high-top sneakers.

"Oops! Sorry!" Penny looked mildly repentant. "Guess that means you're not single after all, huh?" She gave a bounce of frustration on the balls of her feet. "New plan, Penny. What to do, what to do..."

"Ask him." Noah angled his thumb in Vance's direction.

"He's married." She made a face. "I have a real problem that needs a real solution. If you two could be serious for one blessed minute..."

"Me? Serious?" Vance pretended to be horrified. "That's gonna cost you extra."

Doc cut in line to join their small huddle, eliciting a few grumbles from a cluster of guys standing behind them. "Chill." He glared at them. "We'll save you some food." Beneath his breath, he added,

"Maybe." Glancing at his other three squad mates, he grew still. "Whoa! Who died?"

"No one yet," Penny sounded peeved, "though I'm pretty sure this is what it feels like right before keeling over from a stroke."

He snapped his fingers as if just now remembering something. "I knew I should've worn my stethoscope to dinner."

"I don't need a doctor." She rolled her eyes at him. "More like a fake boyfriend for a few days."

"Ah." Doc looked intrigued. "In that case, I'm still your man." He stepped neatly around Noah and playfully crooked a finger at her.

"I'm serious." She glanced worriedly at him. Though he was a good two inches shorter than her, Noah thought they made a striking couple.

"So am I. What's the problem?"

"Sorry to break it to you, but you're not my type," she sighed. "To convince my ex I've moved on, I'm going to need a tall, cocky jerk like—"

He stepped closer to seal his mouth over hers, silencing her in mid-sentence. Palming her neck, he proceeded to deliver a very thorough kiss.

The classmates standing nearby started to clap and cheer them on.

Vance shot Noah a mystified look. "Isn't there a no PDA rule around here?"

"I think so." If Doc and Penny wanted to press their luck, Noah was staying out of it. "How about we circle back to the part where she called me a jerk? Am I a jerk?" He pressed a hand to his chest, feigning outrage.

"All guys are jerks," Vance assured without missing a beat. He was glaring in Doc's direction. "You think he's trying to get himself kicked out?"

"No idea." Noah doubted any of his squad mates would be separated from the training center that easily. They were too valuable. However, he wasn't planning on testing that theory any time soon. "Uh-oh." He angled his head at the two officials barreling in their direction.

"Trainee Peterson," one of them barked.

Doc reluctantly relinquished his hold on Penny, scowling at the interruption.

"We're going to need you to come with us."

"Yes, sir." Giving them a mock salute, Doc swaggered after them, grinning broadly over his shoulder at his classmates.

Penny stared after him, looking stricken. "What have I done?" she cried in a low voice.

"Worst-case scenario, you got a classmate kicked out of the training center," Vance informed her cheerfully.

"I'm such a horrible person," she moaned. "I was actually only joking about the fake boyfriend thing. What was Doc thinking?" She seemed at a loss for words.

"Nobody forced him to kiss you," Vance

returned brusquely. "He did it because he wanted to. Trust me."

"That's not making me feel any less awful right now." She sounded close to weeping. "I didn't even know his real name until those goons showed up. I still don't know his first name."

"It's Simon," he supplied blandly. "Simon Peterson. He started off as a foreign exchange student from Israel and liked it here so much that he stayed."

"Wow! I had no idea." Penny intoned softly, looking more worried than ever on his behalf. "Listen, ah, if you'll excuse me. I should probably go waylay Captain Downs. If anyone can talk Doc out of whatever trouble he's gotten himself in, I'm putting my money on her."

Noah couldn't have agreed more. As she walked away, he shook his head at Vance. "Back to my earlier question. Am I really that much of a jerk?"

Vance snorted out a laugh. "You're still hung up on that?"

Noah shrugged. "I went through a bad break-up last year. So, yeah. You could say that."

It was finally their turn to have their trays filled, so there was a sudden lull in the conversation. This evening's menu was steak, baked potatoes, salad, and dinner rolls — served by a trio of grandmotherly attendants in matching white aprons. Clear plastic gloves covered their hands.

"Thank you, ladies. You just made me a very

happy cop. Where's Bill?" Vance's head swiveled in search of the man as he accepted his tray. For a moment, he looked like he might start drooling on his steak.

"He's around," one of ladies responded vaguely. Her salt-and-pepper hair was pulled back in a net and a dash of magenta lipstick covered her papery lips.

"What's that smile supposed to mean?" Vance asked suspiciously. "Is Bill in trouble or something, ma'am?"

"Always." The three women glanced knowingly at each other.

Vance studied them through narrowed lids. "If you see him, just let him know the linebacker from Dallas was asking about him, okay?"

"Sure thing, handsome." The lady with lipstick politely shooed him onward, lifting her gaze to the next student in line.

"Clearly, they know something that we don't know about Bill," Vance grumbled as he and Noah paused to search the crowded cafeteria for a few empty seats.

"You think?" Noah snorted. "We only met him yesterday."

"Just hear me out, man." Vance gestured toward two classmates who were standing to leave. "I sympathize with your dumb stuff, and you sympathize with mine. That's how this works."

Noah guffawed as they moved forward to claim the vacated chairs. "Define *this*."

"Do I have to explain everything to you?" Vance adopted a long-suffering tone one might use to explain something to a two-year-old. "You got my back. I got yours."

"You sure you want to do that for a fellow jerk?" Noah teased.

Vance tipped back his head to gaze up at the ceiling. "Please, God, give me strength." He leaned over his tray. "And bless this food while you're at it, Sir. Amen." Spearing his fork into his salad, he swiveled to face Noah. "Yes. The short answer is yes. I got your back, because that's what cops do for each other. As for where you truly stand on the jerk-o-meter..."

"Jerk-o-meter?" Noah was fascinated by the word. "Is that really a thing?" It sounded like something Vance had made up on the spot.

"I don't know. That's not the point." Vance filled his mouth so full of salad that his cheeks bulged. He had to chew and swallow before speaking again. "As a happily married man, I should probably give you a few pointers. Women don't always say what they mean, bro. You gotta absorb the whole delivery method to get the full meaning out of what they're saying." He gestured with his utensils, outlining in the air what Noah could only presume was the curvy figure of a woman. "Body language, tone of voice, how fast they're talking. All of it matters. Believe me."

"So, you're an expert at this stuff." Noah couldn't resist teasing him. It had been a long, tiring day. He wasn't in the mood for a serious conversation.

Vance made a fist in the air. "Talk to the arm, man." He pointed to the tattoos of his girls' footprints.

"I still can't believe you're the father of triplets." Noah ate quickly, wanting to return to the dog kennel as soon as possible. "Is it hard being away from them?"

"More than you can imagine." Vance huffed out a breath. "That's the biggest reason I'm glad I got selected for Captain Ironsides' special team. She's gonna work us into the ground, no doubt about it, but it'll make the time fly."

"I don't want this training to drag on, either. For different reasons, of course." Noah polished off the rest of his steak. "I've been working a missing persons case that I really hated putting on the back burner for a few weeks. I entertained the thought of postponing my report date to the training center, but my police chief wouldn't hear of it."

"For what it's worth, I'm glad you're here, bro." Vance took a noisy chug of his unsweetened tea. "If anyone asks, I'll deny it of course."

"Your heart is pure gold." Noah stood with his empty tray. "Gotta run, but I wouldn't mind if you texted me anything you hear about Doc's situation. I'll do the same."

"Aw," Vance mocked, pulling out his cell phone. "Are we texting buddies now? Man! Things are getting real." He held his finger over the keypad and waited.

Noah rattled off his phone number.

Vance hit the save button. "You have officially graduated to the contact list, bro."

"Shoot me a message, so I have your number, too."

"Sure thing. Nothing like texting a guy who's standing right in front of you," Vance noted dryly. "Welcome to the digital age."

"It doesn't take much to excite you, does it?" As Noah moved toward the tray drop off area, he tossed over his shoulder. "I triple dog dare you to put me on speed dial. Then I'll know our relationship is really going somewhere."

"In your dreams!" Vance called after him.

JAVA MET him at the door of her cage, clamoring to be let out. There was a sealed envelope attached to her clipboard. *Noah* was carelessly scrawled across it.

"Don't worry, Java. I'm about to get you out of here, darlin'." He stepped inside the cage to hook on her leash and fill his pockets with milk bones from the supply locker in the corner. Before they took off, he tore open the envelope and scanned its contents. The message was short and sweet: *Urban rubble.*

Noah shredded the note and threw it in the dumpster outside the kennel. Despite his growing anticipation about meeting up with Farrah, he didn't waste the opportunity to put Java through her paces again. Like the evening before, he had her sit, stay, and heel all the way to the open field alongside the urban rubble site.

She wagged her tail wildly each time he rewarded her with a milk bone.

"Careful there, my little coffee-colored friend," he warned for the umpteenth time. "You keep that up, and you're gonna wag it clean off."

"Is that any way to talk to a lady?" a female voice mocked.

Noah would've recognized Farrah's soft, throaty alto anywhere. What a welcome sound! She walked his way in a pale blue and white plaid shirt tucked loosely into faded jeans. A pair of beige cowgirl boots hugged her calves. Instead of the usual ponytail, her hair cascaded around her shoulders. Several strands danced against her cheeks in the evening breeze.

She was so lovely that Noah was momentarily at a loss for words. To cover his tongue-tied state, he withdrew one of Java's blue balls from his pocket, waved it at her, and threw it as hard as he could.

"No," he said quietly when he could finally

speak again. "It's no way to talk to a lady. It would probably make more sense to tell her how beautiful she is tonight."

Farrah stepped closer. "You don't clean up so bad yourself, cowboy." She pretended to sniff the air. "You smell better, too."

"Huh." He crossed his arms as he regarded her. "Didn't realize you were downwind of me today."

She wrinkled her nose at him. "We all smelled pretty awful by the end of the training. I could barely stand my own stench."

"Didn't notice." He caught her gaze and held it. "Guess I was a little distracted by...other things."

She caught her lower lip between her teeth. "What are we doing, Noah?"

"If I had it my way, we'd be enjoying a nice quiet dinner somewhere else. Anywhere but here." He watched the color in her cheeks deepen at his words.

Java came dashing back in their direction, ears flat against her head. She happily deposited the ball in Noah's hand and waited for his next move. He tossed it in the air and caught it a few times, just to tease her. Then he threw it across the field again as hard as he could. She shot after it.

"You're really good together," Farrah mused, staring after her.

"Probably because some hot maid gave me a few pointers on my first night here." Noah loved the way the breeze was tousling her hair. He wished he could reach out and tuck the loose strands behind her ears — and maybe wrap one around his finger and give it a tug. Someone might see them, though, and he wasn't about to muck up her internship with a PDA infraction.

"Are you disappointed that I'm not really Bloom?" she inquired in a low voice

He was incredulous that she felt the need to ask. "Do I look disappointed?"

"No." Her brow remained wrinkled in concern. "But you're only going to be at the training center for a month. Then you'll be heading back to Houston, and I'll be staying here."

The offhand way she spoke about Houston verified that she had no inkling of her real identity. He'd suspected as much. "Is that your way of saying no to a long-distance relationship?" He'd never been a beat-around-the-bush kind of guy. Plain speaking came so much easier to him.

"It's hard to turn down a guy who hasn't gotten around to asking me out yet," she retorted in a shy voice.

"Will you be my girl, Bloom?"

"You're really hung up on her, aren't you?"

"That's not an answer."

"Yes. I'm willing to give it a try if you are."

"Thanks." Relief flooded him at her words. "And, yes. I'm really hung up on you." It was all he could do not to reach for her hand. He wanted to lace his fingers through hers and walk hand-in-hand with her across the grassy field. But tonight, he would have to content himself with having her gorgeous alto voice surround him like a caress.

"I'm a little hung up on you, too," she returned softly.

"Only a little?" He raised and lowered his eyebrows at her.

"I'm not the only female who's hung up on you around here." She smiled as Java came barreling back in their direction. "You managed to win the heart of this lovely tigress in short order. I'm impressed."

"High praise indeed from an Animal Behaviorist." Since Java needed the exercise, he threw the blue ball again while his thoughts skipped ahead to his return to Houston. It might be time to finally rent a real house, one with a yard.

"I call it like I see it. The two of you formed a bond quicker than usual."

"Guess the timing was right." He cast a sideways glance at Farrah. "We both needed a family. Now we have each other. What about you?"

She looked surprised. "You already met my mom. She's a real firecracker, isn't she?"

"Like mother, like daughter." He was hoping to learn more about her family. "Is it just the two of you?"

She nodded. "Yeah. My dad died when I was little. I have no memory of him, and Mom never remarried. We moved around a lot, so she could take various jobs. Then she started her own business and put down roots here."

"Is that what you plan to do after your internship? Put down roots here?"

Farrah looked uncertain. "I truly don't know. It's something I'm praying about."

He liked the sound of that. It was becoming rarer and rarer to meet folks with good old fashioned principles, especially those his age. "Did He give you any answers yet?"

"Not yet. I'll admit that part of me wants to see the world, while the other part of me doesn't want to leave Mom. I'm all she has left."

Maybe not. He studied her for a moment and decided to take the plunge. "Who knows? Maybe you're the long-lost relative of some rich-as-sin oil tycoon or something."

"Right." Farrah rolled her eyes. "If only."

"So, it would be a good thing?"

"You're kidding, right?" She shot him an incredulous look. "If that ever happens, the first thing I'll do is retire Mom. Then we would pull up the proverbial tent pegs and go anywhere we wanted."

"Like Houston?" He winked at her.

CHAPTER 7: THE MOM SCARE

FARRAH

For the entire first week of her internship, Farrah stayed at her assigned cabin on Instructor's Row. It wasn't the official name of the street, but that's what most people called it. She fell into the habit of making a quick call to her mother every evening right before she began her two-hour cleaning shift. It was the only time she could carve out for a chat. By the time Saturday evening rolled around, she was mindlessly exhausted. If she didn't catch up on her sleep soon, she was going to collapse.

She locked her office in the kennel and headed back to the main building to knock on Captain Alicia Downs' door. They'd scheduled one final debriefing meeting for the week.

"Come in," the captain called cheerfully. When Farrah cracked open the door, she beckoned for her to enter. "I thought that sounded like your knock."

She pointed at the pair of plaid upholstered chairs in front of her desk. "Have a seat, and tell me what's on your mind."

"Very little, ma'am," Farrah confessed, muffling a yawn. "I'm so tired that my thoughts have all but stopped."

"Coffee?" the captain asked.

"Yes, please." Anything to keep her eyelids open a little longer. She watched as her boss swiveled around in her leather chair to the beverage bar behind her desk. It took less than a minute to brew a fresh cup that filled the room with the enticing scent of hazelnut and chocolate.

"It felt like a successful week from my perspective, ma'am." Farrah took a sip of the hot, soothing beverage. "I hope you feel the same. I remain open to all criticisms, corrections, and recommendations for improvement, of course."

"I have zero complaints about your work." The captain's tone was matter-of-fact. "I wish I could say the same for Doc." Her lips twisted with irritation. "Although the powers-that-be let him finish out the week, I'm still worried they plan to lower the boom on him once they finish their investigation. It was a blatant act of PDA, hard for even me to defend."

"It'll be a shame if they let him go." Farrah stared blurry-eyed into her cup of coffee. "He only did it to protect a classmate."

"What?" The captain threw down the ink pen she'd just picked up.

"Oh." Farrah must be even more tired than she realized. "I thought you knew, ma'am."

"About…" her boss prodded in an irritable voice.

"About why Doc kissed Penny."

"Get to the point!"

"Penny's ex is a classmate here. She was upset about the way he was pressuring her to get back together, so Doc made a scene in the cafeteria to put a stop to it once and for all."

"Who is her ex, and was he acting inappropriately?"

"I have no idea, ma'am." It was true. Noah didn't seem to know the name of the guy, either.

"I'm assuming your source is Police Detective Noah Zeller?"

"Who else, ma'am?" Farrah was grateful to discover she was too tired to blush. "He's like their unofficial squad leader or something."

"The two of you seem to be spending a lot of time together," her boss muttered.

Farrah shrugged. "I'm outside a lot, and I believe it was your suggestion for him to spend every available second training Java."

"Training he just happens to conduct in the field next to the urban rubble, where you spend each evening setting up the next day's training session."

Farrah shrugged again. "I hear you, but he's not

breaking any rules, so I didn't feel the need to run him off." Quite the opposite. It had been her suggestion for him to train at that exact spot.

"I appreciate the information about Doc." The captain drummed her fingers on her desk. "I'll look into it. Hopefully, it'll be enough to get him off the hook."

"Thank you for having his back." Farrah couldn't stand the thought of anyone in their squad being separated from the training center.

"One squad. We stick together." The captain offered one of her rare smiles. "Why don't you get out of here?" she suggested, eyeing Farrah curiously.

"And go where?" Farrah was confused.

"Home," Alicia Downs said flatly. "Sleep in your own bed tonight, and don't come back until staff check-in time tomorrow evening."

It was a tempting offer. "I can't," Farrah confessed ruefully.

"Why not?" Her boss frowned at her computer screen, looking mildly distracted. "You're not a prisoner here, you know."

"I have to cover the Bloom Where Your Planted ten to midnight shift," Farrah reminded, muffling another yawn.

"What tasks are on your cleaning schedule this evening?"

"The Auditorium." It was too important of a room to skip. "The floors need to be vacuumed and the wall sconces dusted." There were literally dozens of them. It required standing on a stepladder to reach each one.

"Consider it done. Now get out of here." Alicia Downs returned her attention to her computer screen.

"What?" Farrah stammered. "Who is going to—?"

"That was a direct order, Intern Carmichael," the captain interrupted coolly. She pointed at the door. "You're dismissed."

"Yes, ma'am." Farrah was too tired to argue. She carried her cup to the tiny kitchenette in the waiting area outside the captain's office, dumped the rest of her coffee in the sink, and disposed of the cup. After a quick deliberation, she opted to skip returning to her cabin in lieu of heading straight to her mother's van. The half a cup of coffee she'd consumed had given her a much-needed jolt of energy. Hopefully, it would last long enough to get her home.

It felt like years since she'd last driven from the parking lot. She dialed her mother on the way home.

Nancy Carmichael picked up on the first ring, making Farrah wonder guiltily if she'd been waiting by the phone. Which, of course, she had. There wasn't much else for a middle-aged woman with a broken ankle to do, other than watch television.

"Baby!" her mother crowed into the mouthpiece. "How's my favorite Animal Behaviorist?"

"I plead the fifth," Farrah joked.

"Not with your mama you won't." Her mother's swift rebuttal brought a tired smile to Farrah's lips. "So, start talking. I want to know everything about your internship, and I mean everything. All the cute guys you've met. All the—"

"Okay, okay!" Farrah didn't want to have this conversation over the phone. "If you insist on knowing everything that's going on in my life, how about we do a girls' sleepover tonight?"

Her mother's whoop of delight filled the van. Then she grew quiet. "Wait a sec! If you're coming home, please assure me you didn't get fired or something."

"Mom!" *Have a little faith, will ya?*

"What? I worry about you. It's my right."

"It's also my right to visit my favorite mom every chance I get. I'm not a prisoner at the training center." Her boss had been quick to remind her of that.

"What about your cleaning shift?" her mother asked worriedly. "Believe me, there's nothing more in the world I'd like than to spend the evening with you, but—"

"Got it covered," Farrah assured, "and I'm already on my way there, so you'd better get that popcorn going."

HER MOTHER WAS AS GIGGLY AS a high school girl when Farrah walked through the front door. She propped her crutches against the doorway leading to the kitchen and hopped her way across the living room on one foot.

"Baby!" she cried, stretching out her arms.

"Holy cow, Mom!" Farrah threw the van keys in the wooden bowl by the door and flew in her direction. "What are you doing?" she scolded, wrapping her mother in a tight embrace. "Those crutches weren't just a suggestion from your doctor friend."

"They're a pain in my patoot is what they are," her mother fumed. She shot a ferocious frown across the room at them. "I've never felt so tied down and helpless in all my life."

"It's only for a few more weeks," Farrah soothed, allowing her mother to lean on her as they moved back toward her crutches. She suspected part of her mother's frustration stemmed from the fact that they weren't accustomed to being apart like this. Even during her college years, Farrah had commuted from home.

"Just let me crab for a moment," her mother sighed, reaching grudgingly for her crutches. "Between you being gone and me being homebound, I haven't even been able to complain properly."

"You have Snitch," Farrah reminded, glancing around them and wondering why the cocker spaniel wasn't barking his usual greeting.

"You know what I mean," her mother grumbled, hobbling back to the kitchen on her crutches.

"Where is he?" Farrah couldn't see hide nor hair of him anywhere.

"Getting a break from my crankiness. Helen next door offered to take him to the groomer with her brood."

"That was sweet of her." While her mother stood vigil over her prized movie popcorn machine, Farrah opened cabinet doors to retrieve their favorite red and white striped popcorn bowls. She set them on a wooden tray and made two steaming cups of coffee — medium roast with a dollop of vanilla creamer for her mother and chocolate hazelnut with twice the amount of vanilla creamer for herself.

"Shoot!" Nancy Carmichael eyed her daughter as she mixed their beverages, just the way they liked them. "It just hit me how much my coffee creamer bill will go down after you move out for good." Her expression turned stricken, and she promptly burst into tears.

"Omigosh, Mom!" Farrah abandoned her tray to move around the center island. "I know it's been a hard week." It had been hard on Farrah's end, too. She was mindlessly exhausted. However, sleep would have to wait. Her mom was in desperate need of some mother-daughter time.

"It's not just that." Her mother shook her head,

glancing away as tears continued to gush down her cheeks. "Things are changing, and I don't like it."

"I know, Mom. Change can be painful." Farrah felt a little like crying herself.

"I'm not saying I would have it any other way." Her mom lifted her arm to wipe her eyes on her sleeve. "I'm stinking proud of you. Proud of your college degrees, proud of the woman you've become. And no matter how hard it is for me to let you go, I won't hold you back. I promise." Her shoulders shook as her silent sobs renewed.

"Hey, now." Farrah circled her mother's middle from behind, resting her head against her shoulder. "You're not losing me. You're never going to lose me. I promise."

Her mother reached down to grip Farrah's hands, which were clasped around her middle. "It's just been you and me for so long."

Farrah felt the warm splash of a tear on her wrist. "Well, you're the only mom I have, so your position in our mother-daughter club is safe."

For some reason, her words made her mother cry harder.

"Come on." Farrah gripped her shoulders and spun her around. Propping her mother's crutches more firmly beneath her arms, Farrah pointed to the living room. "Let's go sit."

"What about the popcorn?" her mother quavered.

"I'll come back for it."

Farrah got her mom situated in her favorite leather recliner near the television and handed her a tissue. Then she dashed back to the kitchen to fill their popcorn bowls. She returned to the living room with her tray and set it on the end table next to her mom. Instead of climbing on the sofa, she took a seat at her mother's feet, remaining as close as possible.

She crossed her legs and reached for her mug of coffee.

Her mother was still dabbing her eyes with the tissue, but she'd managed to get her weeping under control. "I'm sorry for being so crabby this evening. Your first visit home in a week, and I'm the world's worst company, I'm afraid."

"Will you stop?" Farrah stuck her tongue out at her mother. "You've always put up with me through the good times, bad times, and everything in between. That's how this works. We're a team."

Her mother sniffed loudly. "About that, there's something I really need to get off my chest."

"Oka-a-ay." Farrah took a long, noisy sip of her coffee. It was brewed to perfection, thank you very much!

"I know you were stuck being raised by a single parent, but I've done my best by you."

"I've never doubted it." Farrah eyed her mother worriedly over the top of her mug as the first tendrils of fear worked their way through her gut. Something was wrong. She could sense it.

"Thank you. It's just never felt like enough. I've often had to ask myself if I truly gave you the best childhood I could. I mean, we've never had much money."

"Whatever," Farrah scoffed. "I'm old enough to know that money doesn't necessarily equal happiness."

"It sure helps out, though." Her mother's voice was wistful. Her strained expression suggested she was struggling to find the right words.

"Mom, do you have cancer?" Farrah hadn't meant to just blurt the question out like that, but she couldn't help it. If her mother was sick, she had a right to know.

Nancy Carmichael's eyebrows nearly shot through the roof. "What? No! Where's this coming from?"

Farrah's shoulders sagged in relief. "So, all of this," she gestured at her mother with her mug, nearly sloshing coffee on the carpet, "is just you in a bad mood? I truly don't have anything to worry about?"

Her mother rolled her eyes. "I'm fine." She finally reached for her cup of coffee.

"You don't sound fine."

"I am. I'm just cranky." She set her coffee back down without taking a sip, looking distracted.

"You can say that again." Farrah chuckled and took another sip of coffee. "In case you're wondering, I like it here." She waved at their cozy living room. "I like living on the outskirts of Dallas. I love our little cottage. I'm super proud that my mom owns her own business, and I'm thrilled to the moon and back that we managed to put me through college. What else could I possibly ask for?"

Her mother smoothed her hand over her pale pink t-shirt, stopping to pick at a loose thread. "If you're as content with our humble little existence as you say you are, maybe it's because it's all you've ever known. I want more for you, baby. I always have."

"Like what?" Farrah demanded.

"A bigger paycheck, for one thing."

"Isn't that why I went to college?"

"I don't know. Is it?" Her mother raised and lowered her shoulders. "All you've ever really talked about is your love for animals."

"Maybe I've never talked much about money, because we've always had enough." If they couldn't afford something, like a new dress for prom, they made do with something second-hand. It was that simple.

Her mother smiled faintly. "Maybe every parent feels this way, but I just wish I could have done more."

Farrah had no idea what had brought on this massive case of regret on her mother's part, but she was ready to change the subject. Reaching for her mother's bowl of popcorn, she shoved it gently into her hands. "I don't see how you could've done more. That is, unless we happen to have some long-lost, rich-as-sin relative out there that I don't know about—"

Her mother's bowl of popcorn slipped from her fingers and went tumbling to the floor. The fluffy white kernels scattered in every direction.

Farrah stared at her mother in shock as she grew as pale as a ghost. "Okay. That's it." She set down her coffee cup, dusting popcorn off of her jeans as she stood. "You're not well. We're going to the hospital."

"Forget it!" her mother snapped, weakly swatting away her hands as Farrah attempted to tug her to her feet.

"You nearly passed out just now," Farrah cried. "What's going on? For real, this time."

"I could ask you the same thing," her mother retorted. "Talking about rich, long-lost relatives and such. What's gotten into you?"

"I was only joking." It was out of character for her mother to freak out like that. "It's actually some-thing Noah said to me a few days ago."

Her mother's forehead wrinkled. "You mean that police officer I ran into at the pet store?"

"That's the one." Since the color was returning to her mother's face, Farrah slid to her knees to start scooping up popcorn. "You wanted to hear all about the cute guys I've met. Well, he's at the top of my list." She caught her lower lip between her teeth and continued to clean up popcorn, glad that it kept her from having to look directly at her mother. "I really like him, Mom. He, um, sorta asked me out, and I sorta said yes."

"Sort of?" Nancy Carmichael gathered up the popcorn kernels in her lap and tossed two fistfuls into the bowl Farrah had resting at the base of her recliner.

"Yes. We're officially a couple now. There's no PDA allowed at the training center, though, so we won't be going on any dates until after he graduates."

"Isn't he from out of town?" her mother asked quickly.

"As a matter of fact, he is." Farrah glanced up in surprise. "How did you know?"

"I just assumed he was, since most of the students are out-of-towners. Where's he from?"

"Houston."

Her mother made a faint choking sound. "And what exactly does he do for them?"

"He's a cop, Mom. You know that."

"What kind of cop?"

"Oh, my lands!" Farrah exclaimed, thoroughly exasperated. "Do you want me to buy you a gun to polish in front of him the first time I bring him home for dinner?"

"I'm a mom. I have the right to ask this kind of stuff." Her mother sounded a little offended.

"He's a detective. One who specializes in finding missing people. Kidnapped women and children, hostages, people taken for ransom, that sort of thing."

"I see." Her mother seemed to wilt deeper into the recliner cushions. "So, what did he come to the training center for?"

"To polish up on his urban rescue skills. He's in my class."

"Of course he is," her mother murmured dryly.

"What's that supposed to mean?" Farrah was beginning to regret her decision to spend the evening at home.

"It means I'm suspicious about his intentions." Nancy Carmichael stubbornly lifted her chin.

"I thought you said you liked him!"

"I do. Or did," her mother amended, making a face. "But don't you think it's a little odd the way he waylaid you in the parking lot on his first day there?"

"Not really. It was just one of those random things." A really good thing, in Farrah's opinion. "His dog threw up. He saw a lady in a cleaning van nearby. It sorta made sense to come to me, looking for paper towels."

"Then he bumped into your mother at the store a few minutes later, then ended up in your class the next morning, and now you're dating." Her mother sighed loudly. "That's an awful lot of coincidences, don't you think?"

"Call it what you want." Farrah finished cleaning up the final pieces of popcorn. "It feels right to me, Mom. Like Noah and I were supposed to meet. He's a good man."

"I sure hope so." Worry lines creased the edges of her mother's eyes.

"Mark my words." Farrah dove for a stray piece of popcorn that was resting half-under her mother's recliner and tossed it at her. "You're going to end up liking him."

The lines in her mother's face deepened. "We'll see about that."

CHAPTER 8: DANGER COMES KNOCKING

NOAH

Though Noah felt like he was learning a lot in the urban rescue course, it was torture seeing Farrah every day and not being able to pursue her the way he wanted to. It took real effort not to stare at her, catch her eye too often, or hold her gaze too long when he did.

She was, hands down, the most incredible woman he'd ever met. He loved everything about her — her intelligence, determination, sense of humor, keen understanding of dogs and how they operated, and — of course — her beauty. She could turn a pair of black cargo pants and combat boots into a seriously hot combination.

He spoke to her every chance he got, made sure their hands brushed at each opportunity, and spent the maximum amount of time outside in the training fields after hours in the hopes of bumping into her —

which he usually did. By his third week of training, he could see a trend in her performance. She started off the week rested and fresh, but she was worn to a thread by Friday evening. He knew it was probably due to the second job she was working and wished there was something he could do about it. Tired people were more prone to accidents and mistakes.

As usual, they met after dinner in the training field next to the urban rubble site. He tossed his first ball and watched Java take off after it.

Farrah covered a yawn as she set the scent canisters in position for tomorrow's tracking exercise.

The sound twisted his heart. "Is your mother trying to find a replacement for you?"

Farrah yawned again, this time so wide that her eyes watered. "Can you repeat that?" she mumbled.

"Is your mom trying to find a replacement for your cleaning shift?" He tried not to sound as incensed as he felt about it.

"I doubt it, since I told her I'd handle it. Why?" Farrah stepped back to eye the line of canisters in the grass, then stooped to reposition two of them.

"You're exhausted," he pointed out.

"So are you." She smiled tiredly at him.

"I'm a cop. I'm used to being tired."

She chuckled. "I'm not a cop, but I'm used to being tired, too. If everything goes according to plan, I only have about three weeks left of this double-shift stuff."

Assuming she made it that long without collapsing. He studied her in troubled silence, wishing more than anything he could tug her into his arms and just hold her. Or maybe do a little more than that... He was dying to know what it would feel like to have her lips pressed to his.

She sucked in a breath. "Either I'm really tired, or you just kissed me inside your head."

"Good guess." He reached down to accept the ball Java was waiting to deposit in his hand. Then he threw it again, trying not to think of how close Farrah was standing or how easy it would be to close the distance between them and put both of them out of their misery — and probably get both of them kicked off campus in the process.

He scrambled for a new topic to discuss. "Where would you like for me to take you on our first date?"

Her expression brightened. "Now that you mention it, I was kind of hoping to throw you a small graduation party at the house."

"Really?" That sounded wonderful to him. "Should I read anything into the fact that you're ready for me to meet the parent?"

A bubble of laughter escaped her. "You already met the parent. But, yes. It's partly that."

"Partly? What's the other part?" he teased.

"I was just thinking that, after a month of eating cafeteria food, you might enjoy a home cooked meal for a change." Her voice held a hint of shyness, as if she wasn't sure how he would respond.

"You'd be right." He kissed her again inside his head.

"What's your favorite food?"

"Anything, really." He wasn't picky. Java rushed back to drop her ball into his hands again.

Farrah wrinkled her nose at the two of them. "Worms it is."

His eyebrows flew upward. "Except worms." He did an exaggerated wind-up of the blue ball, pretended to throw it, and instead zinged it at her.

Java stopped in mid-stride, thoroughly confused.

Farrah's movements were a blur as she neatly caught the ball and tossed it in the direction Java had been expecting.

"Whoa! You play ball." It was yet another enchanting discovery about the woman Noah was falling for.

"Four years of high school," she supplied smugly. "My scholarship covered my bachelor's degree, which gave Mom and me a little more time to save up for my master's."

"You're amazing." He glanced in Java's direction to gauge how far away she was, knowing he was going to have to end tonight's rendezvous with Farrah early. The desire to kiss her was too tempting.

"Right back atcha, detective." Her lips turned suddenly downward.

"You say that like it's a bad thing."

"My mom thinks it is." Her voice was rueful.

"No kidding!" He couldn't imagine why. He'd enjoyed meeting her mother and couldn't recall any tension or awkwardness in their conversation.

"Yes. She thinks there are too many coincidences in how we met and that we started dating too suddenly."

"Huh." A prickle of suspicion rolled through his gut. If Nancy Carmichael was truly Nadine Carstens, it made sense that she would see her daughter's cop boyfriend as a threat — especially a cop boyfriend from Houston, where her estranged father lived.

"It's nothing to worry about." Farrah waved a dismissive hand. "She just needs a little time to absorb the fact that I'm out of college, pursuing my dreams. She's had to deal with a lot of changes lately."

He was curious about what all Farrah had told her mother about him. "I hope you talked up the finer points of my detective work — how I rescue missing persons, puppies, and kittens for a living."

"I did." She smiled at his reference to puppies and kittens. "I'm not sure how much of it she heard, though. She wasn't feeling well that evening. At one point in our conversation, I thought she was going to pass out. I tried to get her to go to the hospital, but she refused."

Interesting. "I hope she's feeling better now." Noah was more convinced than ever that his theory was correct concerning the whereabouts of the missing Carstens heiress.

"She is. Thank you. Once she ditches her cast and crutches, she'll be even better. My Mom is allergic to idleness. It's killing her to have to spend so much time alone at home."

She watched as Java raced back across the grassy field again. This time, Noah rewarded her efforts with a doggy bone.

"I'm not convinced that my mom has done even half of the resting she's supposed to," Farrah continued. "She's been organizing cabinets and decluttering closets. Oh, and getting ready for some sort of trip. I saw suitcases laid out on her bed last weekend." She shook her head, looking bemused. "Since she hasn't said anything to me about it yet, I suspect she's planning to surprise me."

Noah's heart pounded at the discovery that Nancy Carmichael was packing. He was afraid he was the reason, which meant it was finally time to break his silence. He hoped he hadn't waited too long. Though he longed to bare his soul to Farrah about what was really going on, it wasn't his story to tell. Her mother was the one who needed to have that conversation with her.

"I hate to cut our evening short," he muttered, knowing what he had to do, "but there's something I need to take care of concerning a case I'm working on."

Farrah's gaze snapped with interest. "Oooh! Did you get a lead on your missing persons case?"

"I did." He held her gaze steadily, trying to picture her moving in Bram Carstens' elite circle. He couldn't do it.

She nodded. "I think I'll call it an evening, too. If I head back now, I can snatch a cat nap before my cleaning shift."

He snapped on Java's leash, and they strolled in silence toward the kennel together, each lost in their own thoughts.

When he reached the door of Java's cage, he paused to give Farrah a sideways glance. "See you in the a.m."

"'Night, Trainee Zeller," she returned demurely, glancing at him from beneath her lashes. Moving around him, she headed to her office in the back of the kennel.

He spent a few minutes scratching Java behind the ears and refilling her water bowl. Then he stepped outside her cage and locked it for the night. "Sleep tight, partner."

Java barked in response and wagged her tail a few times. Then she curled up on her wide doggy cushion and laid her head on her paws.

For at least the hundredth time since the start of the urban rescue program, Noah mentally thanked the good Lord for helping him acquire such an experienced dog to train with. Not wanting to get her riled up again, he forced himself to turn around and move toward the exit. He found himself dragging his heels a little as he passed by Farrah's office. He was out of his mind for even entertaining such thoughts, but he was tempted to knock on her door.

As he paused beside her door, it abruptly opened. Farrah stood there, beckoning him to step inside.

After a quick glance around them to ensure they were alone, he followed her into her office. "Is everything alright?"

"There's something I need to tell you." She wasn't smiling as she shut the door behind him and locked it.

"Sure. Anything," he said quickly. Whatever it was, it sounded serious.

"Good." She stepped in front of him. "You're going to have to come closer for this, cowboy."

Closer? He was riveted by the shy glow emanating from her blue gaze. *Oh. Wow!*

He reached for her hands, lacing their fingers together.

She caught her breath as he used their joined hands to slowly tug her closer. Then he dipped his head and lightly brushed his lips against hers. They were as warm and giving as her heart, moving against his as she kissed him back.

The exhaustion from the week slipped away as he drank in her sweetness. "I have wanted to do this ever since our first meeting in the parking lot," he muttered.

"Me, too," she sighed, leaning into his next kiss.

His heart pounded with joy at finally being able to take things to the next level with her. Having their feelings out in the open like this made their relationship feel more real. He still didn't want to rush things, though. If all of his theories about the Carstens family panned out, he and she were going to have some things to work through. Already his brain was leaping ahead to the possibility of convincing her and her mother to move to Houston. For Farrah, it would feel like the first time, since she was a newborn when her mother had whisked her out of town.

He lifted his head to gaze down at her flushed features. "I know we haven't been together for very long, but I'm falling for you." He gently squeezed her fingers. "In case you can't tell."

Her eyes glowed with happiness. "I had my suspicions."

Her choice of words reminded him that another woman was entertaining some very real suspicions about him right now. Suspicions he needed to deal with before they became a problem for him and Farrah.

"I'd better go." He hated ending their little tryst, but he didn't want to get either of them in trouble.

"Yeah, you'd better." She reluctantly slid her hands from his. "Goodnight for real this time. Dream about me."

"Count on it." He unlocked the door and stepped through it, leaving the door ajar. Not wanting to draw attention to himself, he didn't risk any furtive glances around the kennel. He just kept walking. Reaching the rear exit, he stepped outside and dug his cell phone out of his pocket. He'd programmed in the number to the Bloom Where You're Planted cleaning service days ago. With any luck, Nancy Carmichael would be the one to answer.

He mashed the button to dial her number. It rang a few times. Then a woman answered. "This is the Bloom Where You're Planted cleaning company. Nancy speaking. How may I help you?"

"Hi, Nancy. This is Noah Zeller, Farrah's boyfriend. I'd like to talk." He paused a second before adding, "Please."

Silence stretched between them for so long that he feared she might hang up without responding. "When and where?" she finally asked.

"I was hoping we could talk now."

"Not over the phone." Her voice was flat. "I can be there in twenty minutes."

"I know you're on crutches," he protested.

"I know you can't leave campus," she shot back. "My friend can drive me."

"I'll be sitting in my truck."

"I'll find you." She disconnected the line before he could describe the make and model or tell her where he would be parked. Then again, there was a good chance she'd seen him loading Java into his truck at the pet store parking lot. A woman who had been on the run for twenty-five years was no doubt very good at keeping an eye on her surroundings.

I CAN DO THIS. Nancy stared at herself in the mirror, hardly recognizing the pale creature staring back at her. For years, she'd lived in fear of being found out. Now that it had happened, it was time to figure out what came next.

Was Police Detective Noah Zeller's interest in her family personal or related to one of his cases? How long would he keep her secrets? What would he demand in return for them?

It was with trembling hands that she texted Helen next door. *Any chance we can borrow your car tonight?* She hoped Helen would assume she was with Farrah and not question her request.

Her neighbor's response came in seconds. *Absolutely! Do you still have the spare key?*

Nancy drew a shuddery breath. *Yes. Thank you!*

Her friend sent a smiley face emoji. *Tell Farrah hi for me.*

Nancy sent her a thumbs up and hoped that would be the end of it. She reached for her crutches, glad she hadn't yet showered and changed into her pajamas. An hour ago, she'd been toying with the idea of going to bed early, hoping to pass a few worry-free hours in the land of dreams. Instead, she was stepping into her biggest nightmare with her eyes wide open.

"Please, God," she whispered, "give me the right words to say to Noah." Meeting the boyfriend of her daughter wasn't supposed to be this hard. Moms were supposed to worry about stuff like whether the guy's intentions were honorable or if he had a good enough job.

Instead, she was wondering if her daughter's new boyfriend was the beginning of the end of the beautiful life they'd built together here in Dallas. Or if he represented the next biggest threat she would have to face. Or if he would force them to go on the run again.

Nancy let herself out the side door to avoid attracting too much attention too quickly. The street she and Farrah lived on mostly housed retirees. They were better than a whole pack of watchdogs. They knew, right down to the minute, when the mailman would visit and when the trash truck would drive by. They knew who lived on the street and who their most frequent visitors were. At least one neighbor noticed every time a person drove up or drove away.

All she needed was to have the car rolling before her actions were reported back to Helen. By then, it would be too late for her friend to stop her.

Keeping her head down, Nancy moved across the gravel driveway as quickly as she could on crutches. It was pretty slow going. She wasn't as young as she used to be.

Out of the corner of her eye, she noticed a flash of light. *That's strange.* She glanced up at the sky, wondering if it was a streak of lightning. Ever since she'd been stuck at home, she hadn't paid much attention to the weather forecasts. Why bother if she wasn't going anywhere?

However, the sky was clear. The sun was setting on the horizon, casting an orange glow over the houses on the street. Here and there, it glinted off a side-view mirror or window of the cars parked along the curb.

Must have been the sun playing tricks on my eyes. Nancy reached Helen's beige four-door sedan. Unlocking the door, she slid awkwardly behind the wheel and tossed her crutches into the back seat. It felt weird driving again for the first time in three weeks.

Giving a nervous chuckle, she started the car and backed from the driveway. More than one curtain was pushed aside as Nancy rolled down the street.

Nosy neighbors! She gripped the steering wheel harder.

It was a left turn to get to the main road leading out of the neighborhood, then a right turn onto the nearest two-lane highway that would take her to the interstate.

As she was about to make her right turn, a dump truck gunned its motor and sped in her direction. She got the distinct impression that he did not want her to pull out ahead of him.

"Go on!" she groused. "I'm in no mood to drag race a dump truck."

As he drew nearer, his wheel jumped the curb.

She acted without thinking, hastily throwing Helen's car in reverse and backing up. Thank Heavens there was no one behind her, because she didn't have time to look.

The dump truck rumbled closer, veering sharply into the intersection where Nancy had been sitting only a moment earlier. If she hadn't backed out of the way, the dump truck would have plowed right into her.

The driver didn't even slow down. After he cleared the intersection, he yanked the truck back into his lane and kept driving. She stared after him, aghast.

Good gracious! I could've died.

CHAPTER 9: SECRETS UNRAVELED
NOAH

Noah glanced at his watch every two to three minutes, wondering if Nancy Carmichael had lied about her intentions to meet with him. Maybe she was just buying a little extra time in order to load up her suitcases and hit the road.

But, no. That didn't make any sense. She wouldn't leave Farrah behind. Or would she?

She'd already raised her daughter, seen to it that she got a few college degrees under her belt, and watched her land her first real job. An internship at the Texas Hotline Training Center would lead to much bigger things at summer's end. Nancy Carmichael had to know that.

Still, Noah couldn't picture her leaving the one person behind she'd spent her entire adult life protecting. Noah still had no idea what she'd been protecting her daughter from, though he intended to find out. Hopefully, in the next few minutes.

He glanced at his watch again. She'd said she'd meet him in twenty minutes, but that was thirty minutes ago. He debated dialing her number again. However, he hated distracting someone who was driving. It was dangerous out there on the road, and being on a cell phone significantly reduced a person's attention span. In the end, he resisted the urge to call and continued to wait.

Another three minutes passed before a mid-sized sedan pulled into the parking lot. Noah watched in his side-view mirror as the driver stopped to flash an ID at the gate attendant. Then the car cut diagonally across the lot and headed his way.

She's here. His heart thudded in anticipation. A lot of his questions were about to be answered.

The sedan circled around his truck, pulled crossways, and braked with the motor idling.

Nancy Carmichael rolled down the window. Her features were tight and drawn. "Hello, Noah." Her voice held none of the friendliness it had during their first encounter. She was visibly rattled and gripping the steering wheel.

"Is everything okay, ma'am?" He peered through the windows of the car but could see nothing other than her crutches in the backseat. If she was packed to leave town, her suitcases had to be in the trunk.

"What kind of question is that?" She glared at him.

"A concerned one, ma'am. You're the mother of someone I care very much for."

Her lips tightened. "If you know everything about my daughter that I think you do, your reasons for pursuing her could be questionable."

He grimaced. "With all due respect, ma'am, I fell for Bloom, the maid. Not Farrah Carmichael, much less Farrah Carstens. That happened later."

Though Nancy's lips twitched, there was no humor reflected in her gaze. She possessed the same fathomless blue eyes as her daughter.

"Farrah is an incredible person," he continued. "Everything I've ever dreamed of finding in a woman and more. How could I not have fallen for her?"

"Then I trust you'll keep our secret?" Her mother's voice was low and pleading.

He held her gaze. "I'm bound by the oath of my office to find a missing heiress whom her grandfather claims is in danger."

"Or course she's in danger!" Nancy Carmichael's voice was shrill. "Why do you think I've worked so hard to keep her hidden all these years?"

"Honestly? I have no idea." He studied her with concern. "All I know is that two criminal imposters are currently behind bars for attempting to impersonate her and seize her assets."

Nancy's heart-shaped face grew even paler beneath her freckles. "I can't say I'm surprised to hear that. My family's wealth has always made us a target."

Noah could only imagine. In his experience, money attracted criminals like nothing else. Which still didn't explain why the woman sitting in the vehicle next to him had gone on the run with an infant daughter so soon after giving birth to her. He leaned through the open window of his truck. "Is Farrah's father the person you're afraid of?" He studied the case from every angle, and it was the only explanation that made sense.

She drew a sharp breath. "How did you figure it out? I've never told anyone."

"Logic and gut instinct," he admitted. "In order to help you, I'm going to need a name."

"What good will that do?"

"I locate missing people and arrest criminals. If he's broken the law, I will pursue justice for you." It might take time to build a case against him, but Noah would do everything in his power to ensure justice was served.

"You won't tell Farrah?" Her mother's voice was pleading.

"It's not my story to tell. It's yours." He stopped short of making any promises, though. As part of the investigation, he would have to report back to his superiors.

"Her father's name is Bowen Bradley." Nancy Carmichael watched Noah's expression closely.

He stared at her, wondering if he'd heard right. "You mean the CEO of Bradley Shipping?" he asked carefully. It was the same man Celina Manning had dumped him for.

"Not the current one. I'm referring to his father," she corrected in a shaky voice. "He was relentless in his pursuit of me. I was a bit of a rebel at the time and very much enamored by the idea of marrying my father's biggest competitor. Plus, he managed to play on my sympathies. He was a widower and needed help raising his boy."

Noah's case files were full of reports about her wild-hair exploits as a teenager. However, he was seeing a new and different side of her today. "Was it a real marriage?" he asked. A legal union would be a game changer in his current case. It would mean that Farrah was the heiress of not one, but two, mega shipping firms. Her mother's excessive precautions all these years suddenly made a lot more sense.

"I have the marriage certificate to prove that Bowen and I are, indeed, married. He convinced me to keep our union a secret, promising that we would inform my father about it the day I named him as joint trustee over our daughter's assets. By the time I realized the reason he needed my silence, it was too late for my father to stop him." Her mouth tightened. "I'll skip ahead to save you the boredom of listening to me rant and rave about the unfairness of it all. My new husband made one big mistake with me. He was gone a lot right after we married. Too much. As a new bride, naturally I jumped to the conclusion that he was cheating on me. So, I hired a P.I. to look into the matter."

"And?" Noah prodded when she paused.

"I was wrong. He wasn't cheating. Not with a woman, anyway. Boy, did I grow up fast after I realized the kind of man I'd married." She paused again, looking ill.

"Still listening, ma'am."

"The short version is this. I'd unwittingly married the head of an organized crime family. By some miracle, my P.I. got close enough to hear him bragging to his underboss that he would someday be the owner of both of our companies." She drew a deep breath. "Not simply the trustee of our daughter's assets, not the husband or the father of the heirs, but the owner of it all. I knew there was only one way that could ever happen."

Noah did, too. His jaw tightened. After their daughter claimed her inheritance, she would have to die and her mother with her.

"It's true that my father and I had a falling out over a few things," Nancy continued in a feverish voice, "to include my marriage to a man he despised. But that's not the real reason I left town. I left because I had no choice. It was truly the only way to protect our daughter." She briefly squeezed her eyelids shut. "I knew Bowen would never stop looking for us. But as long as we were running, we'd be alive."

"And as long as Farrah is alive," Noah mused, "she remains the legal heir to both companies."

"Yes." Her mother spread her hands. "Now do you see the problem?"

"Loud and clear, ma'am."

"So, what are you going to do about it?" she asked again.

"My job. Can you provide me with a copy of your marriage certificate?"

"Yes, but it's too dangerous to go up against the Bradleys. Trust me. It's a very bad idea."

"For you it is, ma'am. Not for me."

"Oh, come on, Noah! One cop doesn't stand a chance of stopping a crime family that big. If you think for one second that they don't have help on the inside..."

His blood ran cold. "I can only assume you're referring to dirty cops?"

"Of course I'm referring to dirty cops, Noah! Wake up and smell the roses. Not everyone who wears a uniform shares your work ethic."

Though she was scolding him, his heart leaped at her words. "You think I'm one of the good guys, huh?"

She gave him a withering look. "Farrah wouldn't

have agreed to date you if you weren't." She shook her head sadly. "She never had the luxury of being young and dumb like me. Because of our circumstances, she had to grow up quickly."

"What do you mean?" He frowned. "You've kept her in the dark about..." he shrugged, "well, everything."

Nancy's expression grew hard. "I'm referring to the fact that we've mostly lived on a shoestring. I'm referring to how she had to leave behind nearly every friend she's ever made. She was always a newcomer, always a short-termer, never knowing how long we'd be staying at any one place."

"Until now." Noah leaned back against his truck seat, finally understanding why Nancy had stopped running. She was trying to give Farrah the life she'd never had.

"I wasn't being careless, if that's what you're thinking," her mother snapped.

"That's not what I was thinking," he assured her quickly.

"When I decided to put down roots in Dallas, it had been years since the last creeps Bowen sent after us," she explained in a voice that was pleading for him to understand. "All the pursuing and harassing came to a grinding halt after I faked my death. I had every reason to believe he thought I was dead, and Farrah was out of his reach for good. In the months leading up to the car fire, I had spread the word to anyone who would listen that I was going through a rough patch and was considering giving my child up for adoption. Anyone his cronies might have questioned after the fire would have told him that."

Except there had been no adoption papers. Noah's mind raced over everything he had learned in the last half hour. Bowen Bradley must have figured out the truth. Either that, or he'd never been fooled in the first place. Nancy's fake death stunt was his chance to crawl back into the woodwork and let her think she'd won, while continuing to track her whereabouts from the shadows. A true criminal mastermind would realize just how much that put him in the driver's seat. Like cattle waiting in line at the slaughterhouse, oblivious to what was coming, Nancy and Farrah had been allowed to live for the next several years in peace.

The only thing that had changed in recent months was Bram Carstens' health. With how quickly it was spiraling, Bowen must have realized the time had come for his next move. First, Farrah needed to claim her inheritance, though. Noah scratched his jaw, pondering how a criminal of Bowen's caliber would draw his prey out into the light at long last.

When the truth hit him, his jaw dropped. He jerked his head to meet Nancy's knowing gaze. "It's me," he announced in a dead voice. "I'm Bowen Bradley's next move." He pressed a hand to his pounding chest, feeling like his whole world was imploding.

How could he have been so blind? Hector Manning must be Bowen Bradley's inside guy. His nonstop grumbling about how things hadn't worked out between Noah and his niece felt suddenly ominous. Add in all the speeding tickets for her friends that Noah hadn't been willing to tear up and the DUI citation he'd written for one of her friend's boyfriends and...man! That was the real reason Hector had been disappointed in him.

Noah had refused to cross any lines that the man had nudged him toward. The police chief had been utterly unable to steer him away from being a man of honor. *Which made me the perfect patsy to send Farrah and Nancy's way a few weeks ago.*

It was no accident he'd been assigned to this particular missing persons case. In hindsight, it made no sense whatsoever to keep him on the case after he'd been accepted into the Urban Rescue Training Program. It should have immediately been assigned to someone else. But it hadn't, because he was supposed to be the good little cop he'd always been. He was supposed to "discover" the missing heiress and report the good news back to his superiors. They'd only been using him — Hector Manning, Bowen Bradley, and every other dirtbag in their employ — as a pawn to get the bigger chess pieces moving.

Nancy abruptly released her emergency brake and rolled forward.

Noah stared dully at her, assuming she was taking off. He didn't blame her and had no plans to go after her.

She pulled into the nearest parking spot and stopped. Throwing open her car door, she twisted around to retrieve her crutches and stepped out of the car.

As she hobbled around to the passenger side of his truck, his heart leaped with hope. Leaning across the cab, he pushed open the door. She tossed her crutches in the back of his cab, then used his outstretched hand for leverage to climb aboard.

"Drive," she said softly.

"Where?"

"To Farrah's cabin. I certainly can't go back home now."

"Right." He huffed out a breath, knowing he was partly to blame for that.

"How much have you told the powers-that be at the Houston Police Department?" She reached over to touch his shoulder as he started to drive. "Listen. Nobody blames you. Least of all me."

He felt his eyes grow damp. "So much for thinking I was one of the lucky ones who survived the foster care system." He tasted bitterness. "All it did was make me the perfect target. They played into my greatest weakness." He dashed the back of his hand across his eyes. Betrayal like this cut deep.

"Let me guess." Nancy's voice was infused with empathy. "The dirty police chief was like a father to you."

"Yes." Noah's voice was hoarse with regret. "So much so that I'd like to believe he was at least a little disappointed that I didn't fall in line with his plans for me."

"Hey!" Nancy's fingers dug into his shoulder. "It's his loss and my gain."

Noah shot a sideways look at her.

She shrugged. "Any friend of my daughter's is a friend of mine."

He clenched his jaw. "She and I are more than friends."

"So I gathered." Nancy no longer sounded upset by that fact.

In less than two minutes, they reached Farrah's cabin on Instructor Row. As Noah nosed his truck into the driveway behind Nancy's Bloom Where You're Planted truck, there was a flicker of movement at one of the front windows. The blinds momentarily parted. Then the front door flew open. The figure standing there wasn't the one Noah had been expecting.

Leaping down from the driver's seat, he hurried around to assist Nancy to the ground. Then he escorted her to the front porch to face his girlfriend's boss. Captain Alicia Downs' face was an unreadable mask.

He had no way of knowing if she'd found out about him and Farrah, or if she and Farrah had merely been doing a little lesson planning together this evening.

"Evening, Captain." He nodded respectfully at her as he escorted Nancy up the steps.

His instructor wordlessly moved back and allowed the two of them to step inside the cabin.

"Mom! Noah!" Farrah flew, white-faced, in his direction. She studied him for a moment. "You knew," she accused dully. "All this time, you knew who I was."

He shook his head. That wasn't entirely true, but she was no longer listening.

"Yo, there! Noah, my man." There was no mistaking Vance's voice.

Noah scowled as his classmate materialized and leaned in to clap him on the back.

Captain Alicia Downs bolted the front door and snarled, "Stay vigilant, folks. There are a lot of eyes on us right now."

Noah was amazed to discover that Farrah's tiny living area had been transformed into a military-esque operation. "What's going on?" Both Doc and Penny were hunched behind laptops. A snarl of wires ran between them and the other equipment on their folding table.

"We're F.B.I.," the captain informed him flatly.

Noah lifted his Stetson to run a hand through his hair as he absorbed her announcement. "All of you?"

Vance lounged back against the empty fireplace, wagging both forefingers in the air at him.

"No wonder I didn't recognize you from the state playoff game," Noah grumbled. "You weren't there."

Vance shrugged. "A guy by the name of Vance Briggs was actually playing for Dallas that day." He added in a laughing voice, "I had to borrow a real name in case you decided to check up on me."

Noah grimaced. "I take it he's the one who's the father of triplets?"

"Ding, ding, ding!" Vance pretended to ring a bell.

Noah shook his head. His longing gaze returned to Farrah as a dozen questions burned through him. "What's the plan?"

THE HEAVINESS in Noah's voice twisted Farrah's heart. She wanted to stay angry with him for all the secrets he'd been keeping from her, but it was much harder to do so now that he was in the same room.

"Give me two minutes, and we'll start the powwow." Captain Downs disappeared down the hallway to do Heaven only knew what. Farrah didn't even know if Alicia Downs was her real name.

She returned her attention to Noah, noticing how gentle he was with her mother as he helped her take a seat on the sofa. Farrah quickly took a seat next to her mother as he went to fetch a cup of coffee from the Fed's makeshift beverage bar on the credenza. They had literally taken over her cabin during her earlier rendezvous with Noah. When she'd first walked through the door, she'd assumed she was about to be mugged or something.

She couldn't have been more mistaken. Apparently, a whole team of federal agents had descended on the Texas Hotline Training Center in recent weeks to set up a sting operation, one that involved using the long lost heiress to a shipping fortune as their bait — her.

Hugging her middle, Farrah shivered from the coil of dread spreading inside her.

"Here." The scent of coffee swirled beneath her nostrils.

She glanced up in surprise at Noah's voice. She hadn't heard him approach.

"Thanks," she mumbled, cupping both hands around the mug. She was in too desperate need of caffeine to argue about where it came from and who was delivering it.

"Are you okay?" he asked softly.

"Not even a little." She refused to look at him as she took her first sip.

She felt his sigh of regret all the way to her soul

as he took a knee in front of her. "I'm still mad at you." Which didn't explain how close she was to weeping.

"I know." When she set her coffee mug on the end table, he reached for her hand. She didn't pull it away. "I didn't know who you were the day we met. Unfortunately, once I figured it out, it wasn't my story to tell."

She squeezed his fingers, unable to find any fault in what he'd done as the final pieces of the mystery fell into place.

He leaned closer to speak directly in her ear. "You want to know the truth? All of it?"

"Yes," she whispered.

He gazed deeply into her eyes. "I fell in love with a maid named Bloom. That's all the truth and nothing but the truth, so help me God."

As she searched his tortured, red-rimmed eyes, she'd never before seen him so uncertain. "Noah," she breathed. *I believe you.* It was an incredible feeling.

"Say something," he rasped.

She couldn't, so she did the next best thing. She leaned forward to touch her lips to his.

CHAPTER 10: BADGE OF HONOR

NOAH

Everything that had shattered in Farrah's world during the past hour slowly came back together as Noah deepened their kiss. Everything she'd ever known was nothing more than a half-truth, but he was real. The way they felt about each other was real. And for a moment, it was enough.

When he raised his head, his dark eyes were dazed with joy, making her want nothing more than to keep on kissing him. Now wasn't the time for that, though.

"I love you, too." She reached out to touch his cheek. Despite the fact that his evening shadow was showing, along with his exhaustion, his presence in her living room was her anchor.

He reached up to hold her hand against his face a moment longer.

"Alright, alright, alright!" Captain Alicia Downs

sauntered into the room, reclaiming their attention. Penny Jump hobbled behind her, stooped over a set of crutches. They were identical to the crutches propped against the sofa next to Nancy Carmichael.

Farrah's lips parted in amazement as she stared at her and her mother's doubles. A chuckle bubbled up inside her. "I finally understand why my lowly resume made it to the top of your stack." She'd been central to their plans all along.

Alicia Downs had donned a wig the same honey-brown shade as Farrah's hair. It was pulled back into a sassy, wind-blown ponytail. She was wearing snug jeans that were frayed at one knee and a faded plaid shirt tossed over a simple white tank. Penny was dressed in a nearly identical outfit.

"Do we really look like that?" Farrah squeaked in embarrassment.

Vance waggled his bushy black eyebrows playfully at her. "Not one guy in the room is complaining about the view."

She blushed.

Noah gave her another quick, hard kiss before standing. "I'm liking what I see of your plan so far. I'll throw my support behind any plan that keeps Farrah and her mother safe." He lightly trailed his fingers across Farrah's upper arm. "What can I do to help?"

"Exactly what you've been doing." Captain

Downs sashayed in his direction and tipped her face up to his, as if she was expecting a kiss.

"Very funny, ma'am."

"Oh, come on!" Her eyes twinkled merrily. "It's a little funny."

In light of the no PDA rule at the training center, which he was in violation of many times over, there was no way he was admitting anything of the sort. Instead, he changed the subject. "So, it's business as usual, huh? The dumb cowboy cop continues to play the part of the dumb cowboy cop. Then what?"

"If you're looking for sympathy, don't bother." Vance sent a playful punch to his shoulder. "You got the girl, and you're gonna get to play hero during the upcoming sting."

Noah socked him back. "Are you going to read me in on the case, or keep barbing me with your not-so-subtle insults?"

"See, there?" Vance gestured at him with both hands. "You rough him up a little, and he dries his tears."

Penny rolled her eyes as she returned to her computer. "You're such a jerk, Vance!" She propped her crutches against the wall behind her.

"Yep. Men are beasts." Doc leaned closer to Penny to examine something on her computer screen. While doing so, he momentarily rested his chin on her shoulder.

When Penny's gaze softened, Farrah could only

assume the two of them were together. Apparently, not everything about Noah's elite urban rescue team was fake. She couldn't help wondering about one thing, though. "Back when the two of you kissed in the cafeteria..." She shook her head, puzzled. "What was that about?"

Penny reached up to pat Doc's cheek. "Andrew got called to assist in another case. We were stepping him through his exit lines at the training center when the assignment was cancelled."

Impressive. Farrah was amazed at how well choreographed all of their moves had been up to this point. "I'm still trying to wrap my brain around the fact that this whole special training team at the center was part of an undercover op."

The captain smiled. "The Bradleys aren't the only ones with friends in high places. Your grandfather has been calling in favors for months."

"That sounds like my father," Nancy mused from the sofa. "When can I see him?" There was an ache in her voice that Farrah had never heard before. Unless she was mistaken, her mother actually sounded homesick!

"Soon," the captain promised. "Here's how it's gonna go down." She outlined their plan, starting with Noah's next phone call to Police Chief Hector Manning. She glanced expectantly at him. "Whenever you're ready, detective."

Noah didn't budge from his position at Farrah's side. "There's another option," he drawled.

The captain frowned at him. "Not if we're going to bag us a crime family."

"I could turn in my badge and escort the Carmichaels out of town. Rest assured, those who are after them would lose their trail this time."

Dead silence met his words.

Farrah reached up to cover the hand he had resting on her shoulder. "You would do that? For us?"

"Not for us, baby. For you." Her mother gave a shaky laugh. "As much as I appreciate the offer, though, I'm tired of running." She gestured ruefully at her crutches. "Not that I would get very far right now."

"What do you want, Farrah?" Noah's grip tightened on her shoulder.

She tipped her face up to his. "I want justice. I want to meet my grandfather before he's gone. I want my mother to have the life back that was stolen from her. I want it all, cowboy. That includes you."

He nodding, kissing her with his eyes. "Alright, then. Let's make that call." He moved across the room, rubbing his hands in anticipation.

The Feds linked his cell phone to a recording machine right before he dialed.

Captain Downs pressed a hand over her lips for

Farrah and her mother's sake. The two women nodded to acknowledge the request.

"Well, it's about time!" Police Chief Hector Manning's jovial voice filled the small living room. "How's my favorite detective faring at the big bad training center?"

"You have to ask, sir?" Noah made a scoffing sound. "Listen, I have a lead on the case."

"Is that so, Sherlock?" The chief sounded irritated. "I sent you those artist sketches of the Carstens chick days ago."

Nancy's eyes grew round beside Farrah on the couch. *Chick?* She mouthed the word to her daughter, pointing at herself. *Seriously?*

Noah smirked at them. "Sorry for the delay, sir. The urban rescue course is run like a boot camp. Sometimes we don't even break for meals." The lie rolled so smoothly off his tongue that even Farrah was tempted to believe it, though she knew it wasn't true. Noah was such a believable guy when he was spreading misinformation that it was uncanny.

"Boohoo!" His boss sounded bored. "What do you have for me?"

"I've located the heiress. She goes by the name of Farrah Carmichael and has no idea who she really is. Her psycho mother had raised her in complete squalor. You should see where they live," he mocked.

"Harsh." The chief sounded amused. "I like it."

"I could have her in cuffs within the hour," Noah promised. "Just say the word."

"On what grounds?" Hector Manning demanded irritably.

"Kidnapping, child abuse, whatever else you think we can make stick, sir."

"No mercy, eh?"

"She stole her child's identity, her childhood, and her family," Noah growled. "You and I both know she deserves to be behind bars."

"Spoken like a superhero straight from the movies," the police chief mocked. "I'm sure you've got things under control there, Zeller. Even so, I'd feel better if I sent a team to assist you."

"Why?" Noah demanded. "She's a single mom on crutches. The worst thing she'll brandish at me is a broom handle."

"It's a high profile case," his boss reminded, "and she's proven to be pretty slippery in the past."

"If that's what you want, sir." There was a long-suffering note in Noah's voice. "I'll stand down."

"Don't worry, Boy Scout. I'll make sure you get credit for the collar. I've already written up your commendation."

"Appreciate that, sir."

"So, where is the target, Detective Zeller?"

"In the cabin where she's been staying on campus. She's serving as an intern here. Need the address?"

"Nah, I've got the entire staff roster sitting on the desk in front of me." He paused and grunted. "And there she is."

THE POLICE CHIEF'S gleeful tone settled like a lead ball in the pit of Noah's stomach. The fact that his boss was studying the staff's names was further proof he'd known all along that Farrah was living and working at the training center. "Alright, sir. Guess I'll get back to circling the campus in my truck."

"You do that, detective. Our team is on its way."

That's awfully quick. Since they'd been speaking in generalities, Noah couldn't pinpoint an exact timeline. However, it sounded to him like Hector Manning had deployed his team before their conversation. Something was off about that.

"I'll stand by and await your orders, sir."

The police chief continued talking as if he hadn't heard him. "They'll arrive in a chopper that resembles the training center's fleet. Thanks to the air traffic controller we have embedded inside their tower, we'll be in and out before anyone figures out it's not a training exercise."

Captain Downs made a rapid circling motion in the air, signaling to Noah that she was ready for him to wrap up the conversation.

"Roger that, sir. Anything else?"

"No. I'd say everything is going according to plan."

"Glad to hear it, sir." Noah disconnected the line and shoved it inside his back pocket. His gut was still telling him something had been way off about their conversation.

"Here." Vance cupped his hands. "Throw me your keys so I can move your truck."

"I can do you one better than that." Noah grinned, waving his key fob in the air. "It's a remote start."

"Don't do it!" Vance yelled right as Noah mashed the button.

An explosion sounded outside the cabin.

Everyone in the room jumped.

Noah lunged toward Farrah and her mother. "Are you okay?" he shouted.

Farrah stared at him for a moment, too dazed to immediately process what he'd said. She nodded numbly.

"They know you're here!" the captain shouted to him. "Follow me!"

To Farrah's amazement, the captain led them into the kitchen and pushed aside one of the shelves in the pantry. Behind it was a steel door leading to a hidden room. "All the center's buildings have safe rooms," she explained. "Get inside."

Noah scowled at her. "Why does it feel like you're sidelining me?"

"They just blew up your truck," she reminded. "They think you're dead."

The rumble of a helicopter sounded overhead. Bowen Bradley's goons had apparently arrived to fetch their hostages.

"Come on," Farrah begged, tugging Noah's hand. Her mother leaned on her crutches, eyeing Noah with concern.

He hesitated, knowing she could feel it, too. "It doesn't feel right. None of this feels right." He knew he was missing something.

The captain shrugged impatiently. "We don't have any hard evidence against the Bradleys, so we need to catch them in the act. And none of our built-in safeguards will do us a lick of good if the real Farrah Carstens isn't in a secure location."

"I hear you, ma'am." More certain than ever that he was missing something, Noah mentally replayed the details of his conversation with Hector Manning. He had to assume that Hector had known about Farrah's whereabouts for years. And Bram Carsten had been sick for months. What had changed? What made today the perfect day for coming to collect her? While the wheels of Noah's brain spun over the possibilities, he followed Farrah into the safe room.

"Bolt it from the inside." The captain shut the door behind them.

Noah flipped on the light switch as he bolted the door, then turned around to examine their surroundings. Farrah remained at his elbow, gazing with interest at the bottled water, dry goods, and packages of blankets piled on a set of shelves in the corner. Around the perimeter of the room ran a wide bench that would seat at least a dozen people.

No sooner had the two of them gotten her mother settled with her foot propped on the bench than did a second explosion sound. This one shook the ground and brought a trickle of dust down on their heads.

Noah had to assume that both Alicia Downs and Penny Jump had been taken as hostages. So, what was the second explosion for? Scowling, he pulled out his cell phone to surf both the local and state news channels. He didn't know what he was looking for, only that he would recognize it when he found it.

Which he did.

His gut clenched as he read the headline. *Shipping Tycoon Reunited with Long-Lost Heir*. It seemed awfully premature for the news to be breaking. It would take at least an hour before the police chief's team made it back to Houston with their hostages.

Unless...

Noah opened the article and scanned its contents. But it wasn't the words that held his attention. It was the picture that accompanied it. Bram Carstens was standing with his arm draped around a young woman that Noah didn't recognize. She was beaming from ear to ear, while he looked every bit as ill as the cancer was making him. At least that's what the viewers would assume.

Somehow, his enemies had gotten to him. And since he'd publicly claimed the unknown woman as his missing heir...*holy smokes!* The truth slammed into Noah, knocking the air out of his chest.

Farrah and Nancy's enemies no longer needed them alive. They were nothing more than a liability at this point, a loose end needing to be tied off and snipped. Permanently.

He shot to his feet. "We have to get out of here. Now!"

Farrah's blue eyes widened in alarm. "But the captain said—"

"I need you to trust me." His chest pounded with horror as he reached for her hands. "Please."

She scanned his features for a moment, then nodded. "You know I do."

"Thank you." He spun around and moved to her mother's side. "Here. We need to cover ourselves with the blankets." They were an Army green color, roughly the same shade as the grassy field beyond Instructor's Row.

They swiftly wrapped themselves in the green fabric. Then Noah lifted Nancy in his arms. Her crutches would only slow them down.

"Where are we going?" Farrah asked, running ahead of him to throw open the bolt.

"To the urban rubble." In Noah's estimation, it was the safest place to be when the next bomb hit. The computer simulation training room beneath it was covered in roughly two stories' worth of concrete slabs and metal beams. It was as secure as a military bunker.

They exited through the back door of Farrah's cabin and sprinted down the back alley. Adrenaline coursed through Noah's veins as he carried his precious burden. He could barely feel Nancy Carmichael's weight.

The moment he and Farrah reached the grassy field, another explosion shook the area.

"Don't look back," he snarled. "Just keep running." He had no way of knowing if they'd been spotted. All he knew was that they didn't have a second to spare. He kept his mind on reaching their destination and blocked out everything else.

EPILOGUE

Armageddon. It was the only way to describe the state of the training center's grounds after Noah and Farrah had dug their way out of the urban rubble training site. Sirens screamed in the distance, and more helicopters rumbled overhead, as a combined law enforcement team from the greater Dallas area descended on the Texas Hotline Training Center.

Together, she and Noah carried her mother from what remained of the lower level simulation room. Noah insisted on all three of them submitting to a full medical examination. Other than the knot swelling on her temple, Farrah was given a clean bill of health.

The visiting high school JROTC band struck the opening notes of The Star-Spangled Banner, jolting Farrah from her horrific memories of everything that had ensued on the training center's grounds ten days earlier.

"It's time." Captain Alicia Downs nodded at her. The faint glow of bruises remained on her jaw line from the valiant way she'd fought off her attackers. She and her team had the element of surprise on their side, though. The Bradleys hadn't been expecting to deal with highly trained FBI agents in disguise. Thanks to their hard work and bravery, a group of dangerous criminals was now behind bars. Among them were Bowen Bradley and his son, as well as ex-Police Chief Hector Manning and his niece.

"How can I ever thank you?" Farrah murmured. She was still absorbing the fact that her father and half-brother were sitting behind bars — two men she'd never met and hoped she would never have to meet.

"By serving as the best Animal Behaviorist and dog handler that's ever stepped foot inside the training center."

Farrah's lips parted in amazement. "Do you mean—?"

"Of course I put in a good word for you! I couldn't have had a finer intern."

Farrah's heart sank at what the captain was leaving unsaid. She would be moving on to her next assignment soon. As it turned out, she really was a decorated Army officer, a retired one who now worked for the FBI. Farrah hoped this wasn't the last time their paths would cross. She owed the woman a debt of gratitude she would never be able to repay.

Her life, on the other hand, she directly owed to Police Detective Noah Zeller. She couldn't wait to see him walk across the stage. He'd earned his graduation certificate a bazillion times over. Her boyfriend had done so much more than train during his stint at the training center. He had successfully commenced a real urban-style rescue and had saved many lives in the process. He hadn't stopped when he'd gotten Farrah and her mother to safety. He'd run back outside to help evacuate as many of the center's buildings as possible, to include the kennel. There were a few dozen dogs alive today, thanks to his perseverance and bravery.

Normally, the graduation ceremony was a formal affair full of pomp and circumstance. However, the center had received so much press lately for the valorous acts of their students during a real homeland terrorist siege that the audience stood and began to clap the moment the instructors filed onto the stage.

Farrah gazed at the audience through damp eyes, seeking out Noah's face. He was easy to locate, since he was sitting in the front row with the rest of his team. *Our team.* All four trainees had dropped several pounds during last week's immersion exercise that the training center had chosen not to cancel.

With the help of their canine partners, they'd picked their way through the remains of the explosions that had taken place only days before. The very real evidence they'd gathered was right now being used to build a case against the perpetrators in custody.

The audience stayed on their feet while the training center's commander gave his opening remarks. Then broke into thunderous applause again as the graduates began their promenade across the stage to receive their certificates.

The center's officials gave up trying to speak the names of each graduate over the cheering of the crowd. Instead, they flashed their names across the big screen overhead when it was their turn to approach the stage. *Adjust and adapt your strategy.* It was the mantra they'd drilled into the heads of each student for the past month.

Farrah couldn't stop the trickle of tears as Noah approached her and the captain to shake their hands.

I love you, he mouthed.

I love you, too, she mouthed back.

"In case you're wondering," Alicia Downs muttered in Farrah's ear as he walked away, "I put in a good word for him, too. You'll both be receiving job offers soon."

Farrah caught her breath. "Here? At the training center?"

"No. On Jupiter," the captain teased.

Farrah had no idea what a job at the Texas

Hotline Training Center would mean in terms of her responsibilities as the heiress to the Carstens' corporate empire. At the moment, however, she didn't care. If the training center offered her a job, she intended to take it. This was the life she and her mother had worked so hard to build. This was who they were and where they wanted to be.

At the conclusion of the graduation ceremony, Farrah hurried down the steps of the stage to join Noah and his squad mates in the front row. He caught her in his embrace and spun her around and around.

"Congratulations!" she cried joyfully, winding her arms around his neck. "I'm so proud of you!" Not only was she proud of his accomplishments, she was honored beyond belief to have a strong, brave, and wildly hunky cop for a boyfriend. *Watch and weep, ladies!* She seriously felt sorry for every other woman in the room.

"You still want to celebrate over a private meal?" he muttered hopefully in her ear.

"Yes." She kissed his cheek. "How about this evening at my mom's place?"

"It's a date." He kissed her again before setting her down.

They were soon pulled into a debate over whether or not their group was going to meet for lunch at the nearest steakhouse, as opposed to driving to some legendary family-owned restaurant on the other side of the city. Apparently, Vance had been dying to visit there the entire time he'd been at the training center.

Farrah had never darkened the door of such an upscale establishment. She and her mother rarely ate out. When they did, it was usually at a sandwich or coffee shop. Steak meals had always been out of their price range.

Until now.

Farrah peered around Noah's shoulder in search of her mother. She was standing at the edge of the crowd, clutching the arm of an elderly man on an oxygen machine. Nancy Carmichael had finally discarded her crutches in lieu of a thick boot she was wearing for the final stage of her healing process.

Her real name was Nadine Carstens. Farrah wasn't sure if she was ever going to get used to that fact. All her life, she'd known her mother as Nancy Carmichael. The man at her side had to be her father.

My grandfather. I actually have a grandfather! Farrah's heart raced as she squeezed Noah's arm. "It's him," she hissed. She couldn't wait to meet him for the first time. *I have a family!*

He followed her gaze. "Are you sure you're ready for this?"

"I am." With Noah by her side, she felt like she could face anything — her past, her present, and their future. *Gosh!* She could no longer even picture a future without him in it. Her heart belonged to him, forever and always.

And she was pretty sure he knew it.

Like this book? Leave a review now!

Join Jo's List and never miss a new release or a great sale on her books.

Ready to read about what went terribly wrong between Noah's friend, Seven, and the award-winning chef he married?
Keep turning for a sneak peek at what happens when they find out they've accepted jobs at the same prestigious training center right after they go their separate ways in
The Unlucky Bride Rescue!

Much love,
Jo

SNEAK PREVIEW: THE UNLUCKY BRIDE RESCUE

A Texas Ranger who's secretly married, the award-winning chef who calls it quits and leaves him, and the search and rescue program that puts their hearts back on a collision course...

It's not easy being a Texas Ranger; Seven Colburn is living proof of that. He can tell anyone who wants to listen about the long hours, constant danger, mediocre pay, and number of marriages that don't survive his choice of careers, including his own. When an anonymous donor pays his tuition at the prestigious Texas Hotline Training Center, he jumps at the opportunity to bury his heartache in a new challenge. Only to discover his wife has accepted the position of head chef at the same training center.

Tiffany Colburn's mother warned her not to marry her favorite Texas Ranger on Friday the thirteenth, but did she listen? No. Number one, she's not the superstitious nut her mother is. Number two, it was the only day she and Seven could take off from work at the same time. A little over a year later, however, they're living apart, pretending they don't know each other, and contemplating divorce. Maybe her mother wasn't so wrong, after all.

When the first blackmail letter arrives, Seven realizes his scholarship donor has a more diabolical plan in mind than simply funding his summer training. Since the contents of the letter affect his wife as much as him, he's forced to break his silence with her. Teaming up against a common enemy rekindles a spark between Seven and Tiffany they thought was gone forever, making them realize their latest run of bad luck might actually be a second chance at love in disguise.

The Unlucky Bride Rescue
Available in eBook, paperback, and Kindle Unlimited!

Read them all!
The Plus One Rescue
The Secret Baby Rescue
The Bridesmaid Rescue
The Girl Next Door Rescue

The Secret Crush Rescue
The Bachelorette Rescue
The Rebound One Rescue
The Fake Bride Rescue
The Blind Date Rescue
The Maid by Mistake Rescue
The Unlucky Bride Rescue
The Temporary Family Rescue — *coming December, 2022!*

Much love,
Jo

NOTE FROM JO

Guess what? There's more going on in the lives of the hunky heroes you meet in my stories.

Because...*drum roll*...I have some Bonus Content for

everyone who signs up for my mailing list. From now on, there will be a special bonus content for each new book I write, just for my subscribers. Also, you'll hear about my next new book as soon as it's out (*plus you get a free book in the meantime*). Woohoo!

As always, thank you for reading and loving my books!

JOIN CUPPA JO READERS!

If you're on Facebook, please join my group, Cuppa Jo Readers. Don't miss out on the giveaways + all the sweet and swoony cowboys!

https://www.facebook.com/groups/
CuppaJoReaders

SNEAK PREVIEW: ACCIDENTAL HERO

MATT

I can't believe I fell for her lies!

Feeling like the world's biggest fool, Matt Romero gripped the steering wheel of his white Ford F-150. He was cruising up the sunny interstate toward Amarillo, where he had an interview in the morning; but he was arriving a day early to get the lay of the land. Well, that was partly true, anyway. The real reason he couldn't leave Sweetwater, Texas fast enough was because *she* lived there.

It was one thing to be blinded by love. It was another thing entirely to fall for the stupidest line in a cheater's handbook.

Cat sitting. I actually allowed her to talk me into cat sitting! Or house sitting, which was what it actually amounted to by the time he'd collected his fiancée's mail and carried her latest batch of Amazon deliveries inside. All of that was in addition to feeding and watering her cat and scooping out the litter box.

It wasn't that he minded doing a favor now and then for the woman he planned to spend the rest of his life with. What he minded was that she wasn't in New York City doing her latest modeling gig, like she'd claimed. *Nope.* Nowhere near the Big Apple. She'd been shacked up with another guy. In town. Less than ten miles away from where he'd been cat sitting.

To make matters worse, she'd recently talked Matt into leaving the Army — for her. Or *them*, she'd insisted. A bittersweet decision he'd gladly made, so they could spend more quality time together as a couple. So he could give her the attention she wanted and deserved. So they could have a real marriage when the time came.

Unfortunately, by the time he'd finished serving his last few months of duty as an Army Ranger, she'd already found another guy and moved on. She hadn't even had the decency to tell him! If it wasn't for her own cat blowing her cover, heaven only knew when he would've found out about her unfaithfulness. Two days before their wedding, however, on that fateful cat sitting mission, Sugarball had knocked their first-date picture off the coffee table, broken the glass, and revealed the condemning snapshot his bride-to-be had hidden beneath the top photo. One of her and her newest boyfriend.

And now I'm single, jobless, and mad as a—

The scream of sirens jolted Matt back to the present. A glance in his rearview mirror confirmed his suspicions. He was getting pulled over. *For what?* A scowl down at his speedometer revealed he was cruising at no less than 95 mph. *Whoa!* It was a good twenty miles over the posted speed limit. *Okay, this is bad.* He'd be lucky if he didn't lose his license over this — his fault entirely for driving distracted without his cruise control on. *My day just keeps getting better.*

Slowing and pulling his truck to the shoulder, he coasted to a stop and waited. And waited. And waited some more. A peek at his side mirror showed the cop was still sitting in his car and talking on his phone. *Give me a break.*

To ease the ache between his temples, Matt reached for the red cooler he'd propped on the passenger seat and dragged out a can of soda. He popped the tab and tipped it up to chug down a much-needed shot of caffeine. He hadn't slept much the last couple of nights. Sleeping in a hotel bed wasn't all that restful. Nor was staying in a hotel in the same town where his ex lived. His very public figure of an ex, whose super-model figure appeared in all too many commercials, posters, magazine articles, and online gossip rags.

Movement in his rearview mirror caught his attention. He watched as the police officer finally opened his door, unfolded his large frame from the front seat of his black SUV, and stood. But he continued talking on his phone. *Are you kidding me?* Matt swallowed a dry chuckle and took another swig of his soda. It was a good thing he'd hit the road the day before his interview at the Pantex nuclear plant. The way things were going, it might take the rest of the day to collect his speeding ticket.

By his best estimate, he'd reached the outskirts of Amarillo, maybe twenty or thirty miles out from his final destination. He'd already passed the exit signs for Hereford. Or the beef capital of the world, as the small farm town was often called.

He reached across the dashboard to open his glove compartment and fish out his registration card and proof of insurance. There was going to be no talking his way out of this one, unless the officer happened to have a soft spot for soldiers. He seriously doubted any guy in blue worth his spit would have much sympathy for someone going twenty miles over the speed limit, though.

Digging for his wallet, he pulled out his driver's license. Out of sheer habit, he reached inside the slot where he normally kept his military ID and found it empty. *Right.* He no longer possessed one, which left him with an oddly empty feeling.

He took another gulp of soda and watched as the officer finally pocketed his cell phone. *Okay, then. Time to get this party started.* Matt chunked his soda can in the nearest cup holder and stuck his driver's license, truck registration, and insurance card between two fingers. Hitting an automatic button on the door, he lowered his window a few inches and waited.

The guy heading his way wore the uniform of a Texas state trooper — blue tie, tan Stetson pulled low over his eyes, and a bit of a swagger as he strode to stand beside Matt's window.

"License and registration, soldier."

Guess I didn't need my military ID, after all, to prove I'm a soldier. An ex soldier, that is. Matt had all but forgotten about the Ranger tab displayed on his license plate. He wordlessly poked the requested items through the window opening.

"Any reason you're in such a hurry this morning?" the officer mused in a curious voice as he glanced over Matt's identification. He was so tall, he had to stoop to peer through the window. Like Matt, he was tan, brown haired, and sporting a goatee. However, the officer was a good several inches taller.

"Nothing worth hearing, officer." *My problem. Not yours. Don't want to talk about it.* Matt squinted through the glaring sun to read the guy's name on his tag. *McCarty.*

"Yeah, well, we have plenty of time to chat, since this is going to be a hefty ticket to write up." Officer McCarty's tone was mildly sympathetic, though it was impossible to read his expression behind his sunglasses. "I clocked you going twenty-two miles over the posted limit, Mr. Romero."

Twenty-two miles? Not good. Not good at all. Matt's jaw tightened, and he could feel the veins in his temples throbbing. Looked like he was going to have to share his story, after all. Maybe, just maybe, the trooper would feel so sorry for him that he'd give him a warning. It was worth a try, anyway. *If nothing else, it'll give you something to snicker about over your next coffee break.*

"Today was supposed to be my wedding day." He spoke through stiff lips, finding a strange sort of relief in confessing that sorry fact to a perfect stranger. Fortunately, they'd never have to see each other again.

"I'm sorry for your loss." Officer McCarty glanced up from Matt's license to give him what felt like a hard stare. Probably trying to gauge if he was telling the truth or not.

Matt glanced away, wanting to set the man's misconception straight but not wishing to witness his pity when he did. "She's still alive," he muttered. "Found somebody else, that's all." He gripped the steering wheel and drummed his thumbs against it. *I'm just the poor sap she lied to and cheated on heaven only knew how many times.*

He was so done with women, as in never again going to put his heart on the chopping block of love. *Better to live a lonely life than to let another person destroy you like that.* She'd taken everything from him that mattered — his pride, his dignity, and his career.

"Ouch!" Officer McCarty sighed. "Well, here comes the tough part about my job. Despite your reasons, you were shooting down the highway like a bat out of Hades, which was putting lives at risk. Yours, included."

"Can't disagree with that." Matt stared straight ahead, past the small spidery nick in his windshield. He'd gotten hit by a rock earlier while passing a semi tractor trailer. It really hadn't been his day. Or his week. Or his year, for that matter. It didn't mean he was going to grovel, though. The guy might as well give him his ticket and be done with it.

A massive dump truck on the oncoming side of the highway abruptly swerved into the narrow, grassy median. It was a few hundred yards or so away, but his front left tire dipped down, *way* down, and the truck pitched heavily to one side.

"Whoa!" Matt shouted, pointing to get Officer McCarty's attention. "That guy's in trouble!"

Two vehicles on their side of the road passed their parked vehicles in quick succession. A rusted blue van pulling a fifth wheel and a shiny red Dodge Ram. New looking.

Matt laid on his horn to warn them, just as the dump truck started to roll. It was like watching a horror movie in slow motion, knowing something bad was about to happen while being helpless to stop it.

The dump truck slammed onto its side and skidded noisily across Matt's lane. The blue van whipped to the right shoulder in a vain attempt to avoid a collision. Matt winced as the van's bumper caught the hood of the skidding dump truck nearly head on, then jack-knifed into the air like a gigantic inchworm.

The driver of the red truck was only a few car lengths behind, jamming so hard on its brakes that it left two dark smoking lines of rubber on the pavement. Seconds later, it careened into the median and flipped on its side. It wasn't immediately clear if the red pickup had collided with any part of the dump truck. However, an ominous swirl of smoke seeped from its hood.

For a split second, Matt and Officer McCarty stared in shock at each other. Then the officer shoved his license and registration back through the opening in the window. "Suddenly got better things to do than give you a ticket." He sprinted for his SUV, leaped inside, and gunned it around Matt with his sirens blaring and lights flashing. He drove a short distance and stopped with his vehicle canted across both lanes, forming a temporary blockade.

Matt might no longer be in the military, but his protect-and-defend instincts kicked in. There was no telling how long it could take the emergency vehicles to arrive, and he didn't like the way the red pick up was smoking. The driver hadn't climbed out of the cab which wasn't a good sign.

Officer McCarty reached the blue van first, probably because it was the closest, and assisted a dazed man from one of the back passenger doors. He led the guy to the side of the road, helped him get seated on a small incline, then jogged back to help the next passenger exit the van. Unfortunately, Officer McCarty was only one man, and this was much bigger than a one-man job.

Following his gut, Matt flung off his emergency brake and gunned his motor up the shoulder, pausing a few car lengths back from the collision. Turning off his motor, he leaped from his truck and jogged across the double lane to the red pickup. The motor was still running, and the smoke was rising more thickly now.

Holy snap! Whoever was in there needed to get out immediately before it caught fire or exploded. Arriving at the suspended tailgate of the doomed truck, he took a flying leap and nimbly scaled the cab to reach the driver's door. Unsurprisingly, it was locked.

Pounding on the window, Matt shouted at the driver. "You okay in there?"

There was no answer and no movement. Peering closer, he could make out the still form of a woman. Blonde, pale, and curled to one side. The only thing holding her in place was the snarl of a seatbelt around her waist. A trickle of red ran across one cheek.

Matt's survival training kicked in. Crouching over the side of the truck, he quickly assessed the damage to the windshield and decided it wasn't enough to make it the best entry point. *Too bad.* Because his only other option was to shower the driver with glass. *Sorry, lady!* Swinging a leg, he jabbed the back edge of his boot heel into the edge of the glass, nearest the lock. His luck held when he managed to pop a fist-sized hole instead of shattering the entire pane.

Reaching inside, he unlocked the door and pulled it open. The next part was a little trickier, since he had to reach down, *way* down, to unbuckle the woman and catch her weight before she fell. It would've been easier is she was conscious and able to follow instructions. Instead, he was going to have to rely on his many years of physical training.

I can do this. I have to do this. An ominous hiss of steam and smoke from beneath the front hood stiffened his resolve and made him move faster.

"Come on, lady," Matt muttered, releasing her seatbelt and catching her. With a grunt of exertion, he hefted her free of the mangled cab. Then he half-slid, half hopped to the ground with her in his arms and took off at a jog.

Clad in jeans, boots, and a pink and white plaid

shirt, she was lighter than he'd been expecting. Her upper arm, that his left hand was cupped around, felt desperately thin despite her baggy shirt. It was as if she'd recently been ill and lost a lot of weight. One long, strawberry blonde braid dangled over her shoulder, and a sprinkle of freckles stood out in stark relief against her pale cheeks.

He hoped like heck she hadn't hit her head too hard on impact. Visions of various traumatic brain injuries and their various complications swarmed through his mind, along with the possibility he'd just moved a woman with a broken neck. *Please don't be broken.*

Since the road was barricaded, he carried the woman to the far right shoulder and up a grassy knoll where Officer McCarty was depositing the other injured victims. A dry wind gusted, sending a layer of fine-grain dust in their direction, along with one prickly, rolling tumbleweed. About twenty yards away was a rocky canyon wall that went straight up, underscoring the fact that there really hadn't been any way for the hapless van and pickup drivers to avoid the collision. They'd literally been trapped between the canyon and oncoming traffic.

An explosion ricocheted through the air. Matt's back was turned to the mangled pile of vehicles, but the blast shook the ground beneath him. On pure instinct, he dove for the grass, using his body as a shield over the woman in his arms. He used one hand to cradle her head against his chest and his other to break their fall as best as he could.

A few people cried out in fear, as smoke billowed around them, blanketing the scene. For the next few minutes, it was difficult to see much, and the wave of ensuing heat had a suffocating feel to it. The woman beneath Matt remained motionless, though he was pretty sure she mumbled something a few times. He crouched over her, keeping her head cradled beneath his hand. A quick exam determined she was breathing normally, but she was still unconscious. He debated what to do next.

The howl of a fire engine sounded in the distance. His shoulders slumped in relief. Help had finally arrived. More sirens blared, and the area was soon crawling with fire engines, ambulances, and paramedics with stretchers. One walked determinedly in his direction through the dissipating smoke.

"What's your name, sir?" the EMT worker inquired in calm, even tones. Her chin-length dark hair was blowing nearly sideways in the wind. She shook her head to knock it away, revealing a pair of snapping dark eyes that were full of concern.

"I'm Sergeant Matt Romero," he informed her out of sheer habit. *Well, maybe no longer the sergeant part.* "I'm fine. This woman is not. I don't know her name. She was unconscious when I pulled her from her truck."

As the curvy EMT stepped closer, Matt could read her name tag. *Corrigan.* "I'm Star Corrigan, and I'll do whatever I can to help." Her forehead wrinkled in alarm as she caught sight of the injured woman's face. "Omigosh! Bree?" Tossing her red medical bag on the ground, she slid to her knees beside them. "Oh, Bree, honey!" she sighed, reaching for her pulse.

"I-I..." The woman stirred. Her lashes fluttered a few times against her cheeks. Then they snapped open, revealing two pools of the deepest blue Matt had ever seen. They held a very glazed-over look in them as they latched onto his face. "Don't go," she pleaded with a hitch to her voice that might've been due to emotion or the amount of smoke she'd inhaled.

Either way, it tugged at every one of his heartstrings. There was a lost ring to her voice, along with an air of distinct vulnerability, that made him want to take her in his arms again and cuddle her close.

"I won't," he promised huskily, hardly knowing what he was saying. He probably would have said anything to make the desperate look in her eyes go away.

"I'm not loving her heart rate." Star produced a penlight and flipped it on. Shining it in one of her friend's eyes, then the other, she cried urgently, "Bree? It's me, Star Corrigan. Can you tell me what happened, hon?"

A shiver worked its way through Bree's too-thin frame. "Don't go," she whispered again to Matt, before her eyelids fluttered closed. Another shiver worked its way through her, despite the fact she was no longer conscious.

"She's going into shock." Star glanced worriedly over her shoulder. "Need a stretcher over here!" she called sharply. One was swiftly rolled their way.

Matt helped her lift and deposit their precious burden aboard.

"Can you make it to the hospital?" Star asked as he helped push the stretcher toward the nearest ambulance. "Bree seemed pretty intent on having you stay with her."

Matt's brows shot up in surprise. "Uh, sure." As far as he could tell, he'd never laid eyes on the injured woman before today. More than likely she'd mistaken him for someone else. He didn't mind helping out, though. *Who knows?* Maybe he could give her medical team some information about the rescue that they might find useful in her treatment.

Or maybe he was just drawn to the fragile-looking Bree for reasons he couldn't explain. Whatever the case, he found he wasn't in a terrible hurry to bug out of there. He had plenty of extra time built into his schedule before his interview tomorrow. The only real task he had left for the day was finding a hotel room once he reached Amarillo.

"I just need to let Officer McCarty know I'm

leaving." Matt shook his head sheepishly. "I kinda hate to admit this, but he had me pulled over for speeding when this all went down." He waved a hand at the carnage around them. It was a dismal sight of twisted, blackened metal and scorched pavement. All three vehicles were totaled.

Star snickered, then seemed to catch herself. "Sorry. Inappropriate laughter. Very inappropriate laughter."

He shrugged, not in the least offended. A lot of people laughed when they were nervous or upset, which she clearly was about her unconscious friend. "Guess it was pretty stupid of me to be driving these long empty stretches without my cruise control on." Especially with the way he'd been seething and brooding nearly non-stop for the past seventy-two hours.

Star shot him a sympathetic look. "Believe me, I'm not judging. Far from it." She reached out to pat Officer McCarty's arm as they passed him with the stretcher. "The only reason a bunch of us in Hereford don't have a lot more points on our licenses, is because we grew up with this sweet guy."

"Aw, shoot! Is that Bree?" Officer McCarty groaned. He pulled his sunglasses down to take a closer look over the top of them. His stoic expression was gone. In its place was one etched with worry. The personal kind. Like Star, he knew the victim.

"Yeah." Star's pink glossy lips twisted. "She and her brother can't catch a break, can they?"

Since they were only a few feet from the back of an ambulance and since two more paramedics converged on them to help lift the stretcher, Matt peeled away to face the trooper who'd pulled him over.

"Any issues with me following them to the hospital, officer? Star asked if I would." Unfortunately, it would give the guy more time and opportunity to ticket Matt, but that couldn't be helped.

"Emmitt," Officer McCarty corrected. "Just call me Emmitt, alright? I think you more than worked off your ticket back there."

"Thanks, man. Really appreciate it." Matt held out a hand, relieved to hear he'd be keeping his license.

They soberly shook hands, eyeing each other.

"You need me to come by the PD to file a witness report or anything before I boogie out of town?"

"Nah. Just give me a call, and we'll take care of it over the phone." Emmitt pulled out his wallet and produced a business card. "Not sure if we'll need your story, since I saw how it went down, but we should probably still cross every T."

"Roger that." Matt stuffed the card in the back pocket of his jeans.

"Where are you headed, anyway?"

"Amarillo. Got an interview at Pantex tomorrow."

"Solid company." Emmitt nodded. "Got several friends who work up there."

Star leaned out from the back of the ambulance. "You coming?" she called to Matt.

He nodded vigorously and jogged toward his truck. Since the ambulance was on the opposite side of the accident, he turned on his blinker, crossed the lanes near Emmitt's SUV, and put his oversized tires to good use traversing the pitchy median. He had to spin his wheels a bit in the center of the median to get his tires to grab the sandy incline leading to the other side of the highway. Once past the accident, he had to re-cross the median to get back en route. It was a good thing he'd upgraded his truck for off-roading purposes.

They continued north and drove the final twenty minutes or so to Amarillo, which boasted a much bigger hospital than any of the smaller surrounding towns. Luckily, Matt was able to grab a decently close parking spot just as another vehicle was leaving. He jogged into the waiting room, dropped Star Corrigan's name a few times, and tried to make it sound like he was a close friend of the patient. A "close friend" who sadly didn't even know her last name.

The receptionist made him wait while she paged Star, who appeared a short time later to escort him back. "She's in Bay 6," she informed him in a strained voice, reaching for his arm and practically dragging him behind the curtain.

If anything, Bree looked even thinner and more fragile than she had outside on the highway. A nurse was bent over her, inserting an I.V.

"She still hasn't woken up. Hasn't even twitched." Star's voice was soft, barely above a whisper. "They're pretty sure she has a concussion. Gonna run the full battery of tests to figure out what's going on for sure."

Matt nodded, not knowing what to say.

The EMT's pager went off. She snatched it up and scowled at it. "Just got another call. It's a busy day out there for motorists." She punched in a reply, then cast him a sideways glance. "Any chance you can stick around until Bree's brother gets here?"

That's when it hit him that this had been her real goal all along — to ensure that her friend wasn't left alone. She'd known she could get called away to the next job at any second.

"No problem." He offered what he hoped was a reassuring smile. Amarillo was his final destination, anyway. "This is where I was headed, actually. Got an interview at Pantex in the morning."

"No kidding! Well, good luck with that," she returned with a curious, searching look. "A lot of my friends moved up this way for jobs after high school."

Emmitt had said the same thing. "Hey, ah..." He

hated detaining her a second longer than necessary, since she was probably heading out to handle another emergency. However, it might not hurt to know a few more details about the unconscious Bree if he was to be left alone with her. "Mind telling me Bree's last name?"

"Anderson. Her bother is Brody. Brody Anderson. They run a ranch about halfway between here and Hereford, so it'll take him a good twenty minutes or so to get here."

"No problem. I can stay. It was nice meeting you, by the way." His gaze landed on Bree's left hand, which was resting limply atop the white blankets on her bed. It was bare of a wedding ring. *Why did I look? I'm a complete idiot for looking.* He forced his gaze back to the EMT. "Sorry about the circumstances, though."

"Me, too." She shot another worried look at her friend and dropped her voice conspiratorially. "Hey, you're really not supposed to be back here since you're not family, but I sorta begged and they sorta agreed to fudge on the rules until Brody gets here." She eyed him worriedly.

"Don't worry." He could tell she hated the necessity of leaving. "I'll stay until he gets here, even if I get booted out to the waiting room with the regular Joes."

"Thanks! Really." She whipped out her cell

phone. "Here's my number in case you need to reach me for anything."

Well, that was certainly a smooth way to work a pickup line into the conversation. Not that Matt was complaining. His sorely depleted ego could use the boost. He dug for his phone. "Ready."

She rattled off her number, and he quickly texted her back so she would have his.

"Take care of her for me, will you, Matt?" she pleaded anxiously.

On second thought, that was real worry in her voice without any trace of a come-on. Maybe Star hadn't been angling for his number, after all. Maybe she was just that desperate to ensure her friend wasn't going to be left alone in the ER. He nodded his agreement and fist-bumped her.

She tapped back, pushed past the curtain, and was gone. The nurse followed, presumably to report Bree's vitals to the ER doctor on duty.

Matt moved to the foot of the hospital bed. "So who do you think I am, Bree?" *Why did you ask me to stay?*

Her long blonde lashes remained resting against her cheeks. It looked like he was going to have to stick around for a while if he wanted answers.

I hope you enjoyed the first chapter of

BORN IN TEXAS #1: Accidental Hero.
Available in eBook, paperback, and Kindle Unlimited!

The whole alphabet is coming! Read them all:
A - Accidental Hero
B - Best Friend Hero
C - Celebrity Hero
D - Damaged Hero
E - Enemies to Hero
F - Forbidden Hero
G - Guardian Hero
H - Hunk and Hero
I - Instantly Her Hero
J - Jilted Hero
K - Kissable Hero
L - Long Distance Hero

Much love,
Jo

SNEAK PREVIEW: WINDS OF CHANGE

Heart Lake

The cowboy bad boy who broke her heart years ago and the career opportunity that offers them a second chance at happily-ever-after...

While they were growing up, Hope Remington was the darling of Heart Lake, and Josh Hawling was...well, bad news. And now she's returning after ten years of being gone, with a PhD and plans to use her new position to transform their struggling high school into a center for educational excellence.

She soon realizes that her biggest challenge isn't going to be the rival gangs embedded in the student body, although they're a close second on the list. It's Josh Hawling, who has somehow convinced their aging superintendent that he and his security firm partner can coach their backwoods collection of farm boys into a football team that'll make the playoffs.

How is a woman of her refined background and education supposed to improve test scores and graduation rates when her students' biggest idol is a man who spent more time in the principal's office than in the classroom? Even though she feels safer having him on their crime-ridden campus, she's so not looking forward to her daily encounters with his cocky self. Or being socked in the heart all over again by his devastating smile. Or having to finally face her unwanted attraction that might have kindled into a lot more if she'd never left Texas in the first place.

Welcome to Heart Lake! A small town teaming with old family rivalries, the rumble of horses' hooves, and folks — on both sides of the law and everywhere in between — that you'll never forget.

Winds of Change
Available in eBook, paperback, hard cover, and Kindle Unlimited!

Read them all!
Winds of Change
Song of Nightingales
Perils of Starlight

Return of Miracles
Thousands of Gifts
Race of Champions
Storm of Secrets
Season of Angels

Much love,
Jo

ALSO BY JO GRAFFORD

For the most up-to-date printable list of my books:

Click here

or go to:

https://www.JoGrafford.com/books

For the most up to date printable list of books by Jo Grafford, writing as Jovie Grace (*sweet historical romance*):

Click here

or go to:

https://www.jografford.com/joviegracebooks

ABOUT JO

Jo is an Amazon bestselling author of sweet and inspirational romance stories about faith, hope, love and family drama with a few Texas-sized detours into comedy. She also writes sweet and inspirational historical romance as Jovie Grace.

1.) Follow on Amazon!
amazon.com/author/jografford

2.) Join Cuppa Jo Readers!
https://www.facebook.com/groups/
CuppaJoReaders

3.) Follow on Bookbub!

https://www.bookbub.com/authors/jo-grafford

4.) Follow on Instagram!
https://www.instagram.com/jografford/

5.) Follow on YouTube
https://www.youtube.com/channel/
UC3R1at97Qso6BXiBIxCjQ5w

amazon.com/authors/jo-grafford

bookbub.com/authors/jo-grafford

facebook.com/jografford

instagram.com/jografford

pinterest.com/jografford

Made in the USA
Monee, IL
20 February 2023